CW01426078

Space Dragons: Luxorian's Crew

Space Dragons, Volume 1

Veo Corva

Published by Witch Key Fiction, 2024.

First published in 2024 by Witch Key Fiction
Copyright © 2024 Veo Corva
All rights reserved.
This book or any portion thereof may not be reproduced or used in
any manner whatsoever without the express written permission of the
author except for the use of brief quotations in a book review.
All characters and events in this publication are fictitious and any
resemblance to any real persons, living or dead, is purely coincidental.
EPUB ISBN: 978-1-7394742-4-9
Print ISBN: 978-1-7394742-5-6
Veo Corva
Website: https://veocorva.xyz
Witch Key Fiction
Website: https://witchkeyfiction.xyz
Cover art by Dona Vajgand
Website: https://dona.neocities.org/
Many thanks to the supporters of the
Space Dragons: Luxorian's Crew crowdfunding campaign.

Table of Contents

For Merlin. I'm so glad you're still here.

Chapter One

'Humans are a necessary annoyance,' my mother had said to me. A feathered wyrm in her seventies, she'd had three riders in her time and had retired from rig work a decade earlier. 'They're like electricity, or medical care. You've gone too long without one and you're going to get hurt.'

I had wanted to tell her that humans provided the electricity and the medical care, and that it wasn't the same thing at all. I had wanted to tell her that it wasn't that I couldn't be complete without a human, it was that I couldn't be complete with one.

But my tongue hadn't formed the words, and my chest had been tight, and my fire had licked painfully at my gizzard, so I had only nodded and drummed my claws against the slick synthetic flooring. And somehow, a week later, I was at the Lema-dar Tribute Fair being eyed-up by a crowd of humans who had probably never even *seen* a void rig, let alone the dragons that pulled them.

Shining winds, but I hated people, and there were just so many of them here. Lema-dar's vast market-space was clear of the usual stalls of scrappers, crafters, and merchants hawking their wares, and now instead it was all recruitment, which in many ways was less palatable. Children ran down the dusty streets flying flags with the Cosmic Defenders' insignia on it, as if we needed any more warriors in the void than we already had. The sight of the sword flanked by wings made me shudder and fluff up my feathers.

Then there were the crowds around every stall. People looking to sign up with existing rigs, chatting with the human riders while their dragons curled around the stalls. The dragons inputted only when they felt like it and clearly enjoyed the admiring, awe-stricken gazes of the many country hicks that had made the journey to Lema-dar for the spectacle of it all. I watched one dragon, a scaled drake with bat-like wings, flick her long, spade-like tail to the delight of the crowd of human teenagers that had been creeping ever closer. Even the spade of her tail was almost half as large as a human; most adult humans were barely as tall as our forelegs, and scrawny besides.

There were bots here too, scattered amongst the crowd, but none too bothered with us; bots rarely travelled in our rigs, finding more mechanical work instead. They clustered around their own stalls, offering repair and crafting work too complex for human hands, recruiting other mechanics to their businesses.

The press of so many humans and dragons and bots, the noise and stink of it all, was overwhelming. I was lucky that Lema-dar was small for a spaceport town, that the buildings here were simple huts and hab-domes and not the enormous sprawling hab-manors and towering apartment blocks of somewhere like Var-reel, on the other side of the planet.

But it had been fifteen years since I'd had to be at a Tribute Fair at all, and I found it hard to be grateful.

And then, filing in one at a time, the humans were released into our fenced-in area to offer tribute. Only a dozen of them, and of those only six who looked like they had rider potential. The ones with the easy confidence of humans who'd been off-world, who'd flown the void in a rig pulled by a dragon's solar wings. All of them bore gifts or dropped them at their feet; more token than anything, an ancient tradition to win our favour, though nowadays they were interviewing us as much as we were interviewing them.

I sort of hated them.

The dragon beside me raised her crested brows. 'Not many of them,' she said. She was a young thing, barely twenty, at my guess. Feathery, like me, but built on more serpentine lines than I was. I was fat, but had always had a stockier build. More drake, less wyrm, as they say. 'Perhaps I should have waited to get Tribute at Var-reel instead.'

There were three of us. The other dragon, a drake with two heads and thick black fur, looked no older than the one beside me. He looked excited, though. Eager. So did the young wyrm, though she tried to hide it with false scepticism. Her ears were perked, her eyes dilated.

I sort of hated them, too.

Each of the humans introduced themselves loudly, the amp-badges pinned to their chests amplifying their voices. Willem, Rin, Boro...the names all blurred together. As did their tributes, varying from precious gems to baskets of homemade food to blankets woven to a dragon's scale.

I couldn't click my claws against this dirt so I kneaded it instead, digging deep gouges into the dust and gravel that I hoped nobody noticed.

The humans strode forward one by one and offered their tribute to the dragon of their choice. Four humans went to the furred dragon and five to the feathered wyrm beside me. Only three came to me. A relief, in that I hated meeting people and wanted this over quickly; an insult, in that I was an experienced rig-dragon of *fifteen years* and those beside me could only have a year or two of experience at most.

Maybe it was shallow of them. Or maybe they were just being practical, and didn't want to tie themselves to a partner that was already tired of the whole thing. Or maybe it was because I hadn't made eye contact with a single one of them, hadn't fanned my feathered tail prettily or narrowed my eyes in a blink of welcome. But I hadn't done that last time, either, and I had still had the choice of the best rider of the lot.

Who...had turned out to be the worst human.

I didn't want to think about her.

'Lux, isn't it?' said the first human before me. His voice was rough and pleasant, and he had a scrap of beard and silvered hair that had once been black. His skin was a dark umber and his eyes were the colour of slate. He wore a thick leather coat—real leather, from the smell—and had an easy, adventurous look about him. 'I bring you tribute of salt crystals from far Lucen, on the Diamond Belt.'

'I know where Lucen is,' I said. I had been there many times with my former rider. I didn't remember this human's name; Boro or Bara, maybe. I was terrible with names, especially when I wasn't listening.

I had *meant* to listen, but it was hard enough to pay attention when I wasn't already desperately wishing myself home.

'Of course you know,' said probably-Boro. 'You're a dragon of an illustrious career, not one who's barely more than a kit. I appreciate experience.' He gave me a slow smile. 'And beauty, both of which you have.'

I blew hot air out of my nose. 'Beauty doesn't have much to do with being a good rig-dragon,' I said. 'And I am not considered much of a beauty of my kind.'

Boro looked...a little taken aback by this, but that wasn't an uncommon response from anyone I spoke to, ever. He seemed to rally, hoisting his smile like he was dragging a flag up a pole. 'It matters that we get on,' he agreed. 'That we have...chemistry. Your experience is in trade, correct?'

I nodded, as if I needed to confirm it; he'd have read it in my file, just as I should have read his, if I hadn't been avoiding even thinking about the fair. 'Well, so is mine,' he said. 'I rode as crew with Verhalian and Lis Tarven for ten years. We mostly flew the Epicar,' he named a mildly uncommon trade route, 'though we took odd jobs here and there. In my time, I got a feel for good chemistry. And I think,' he smiled slowly again, and winked. 'You and I...we have it.'

'We don't,' I said, almost without meaning to. That wink was primally disturbing to me.

'Opposites attract,' said Boro, putting his hands on his hips.

'People aren't magnets,' I said, mantling my wings. 'And neither are dragons and riders.'

Boro flinched a little. From my tone or my wings, I couldn't tell. 'Look,' he said. 'We're both experienced. I've got a bright, shiny new rig...I think we'd do well together. And...' he lowered his voice. 'As beautiful as you are, you're not exactly a young dragon. Me, I'm looking for a smart dragon. I love the mind. But others aren't necessarily as cerebral as I am.'

What was with this complete change of tack? One minute, he was praising my beauty and experience, the next he was telling me I was too old for anyone else to appreciate? I resisted the urge to bare my teeth at him, but I stood straighter and forced myself to stop kneading the dirt and properly consider him.

He was...I had seen humans like him courting Sar. He was a flirt, used to getting his way through charm, and when that failed by undermining his targets. Sar had always seen right through humans like that, though she had enjoyed their attentions. I could see right through him, too, and I was a dragon and asexual besides. Maybe you could charm some dragons, but you certainly couldn't flirt with *me* and expect to make a good first impression.

'Consider it,' said Boro, pouting up at me with his tiny, flat human face. He left his basket of salt crystals even though I hadn't accepted his tribute; a gesture of wealth that left me unmoved.

I sighed and blew hot air through my nose, and then it was time for the next human. This one was tall and fat and anxious-looking. They were maybe in their late thirties, not so different in age to me. Their blue jacket was much-patched quilt-cloth and their boots were terribly scuffed and so stained that I couldn't have guessed the original colour. Their hair was a short, curly mess atop their head. Black, and their skin a dark gold. A small mech orbited them; a guide mech, from the hesitance of their step and the telescopic cane they tapped before them. They must be low-vision, possibly blind.

If they had tribute, I couldn't see it. I resisted the urge to crane my neck around, looking for it. It wouldn't speak well of me.

They wrung their hands. I tried to remember their name, but it could have been any of the dozens of names they'd all called out at the start. 'I don't really know what to say,' said the human. 'You've read my file. You know what I have to offer.'

I hadn't and I didn't, but I could hardly admit that. I should never have come to this fetid fucking Tribute Fair.

'I, uh...I can't aff—my tribute is personal.' They suddenly snapped into a new sentence, as if remembering a rote script.

I nodded, encouraging them on. Personal tributes were more the stuff of myth than practical reality, but I'd always been a little charmed by the idea of them. Stories of the dragons of old accepting family heirlooms of little value from paupers that later became princes. Fairytales.

The scruffy human before me definitely appeared to be more pauper than prince. They reached under their shirt and pulled a necklace over their head, a small talisman on a string of twine. They held it out in front of them and in spite of myself, I leaned forward to study it more closely. It was a steel disc, like an ancient coin. The surface had been smoothed and etched with a crude flower and some detailing I couldn't quite make out. Writing, maybe. It smelled of them, long-held against their skin.

'My mother made this,' said the would-be rider. 'The Bone Witch has her soul now,' they added, invoking a human death spirit. I thought there was something sad about their voice, about the way it shook. Their mech scanned me, then continued its orbit. It was likely sending them a description of their surroundings.

I decided to take them in a little more deliberately. No swagger or confidence from this one. Their accent had been strange; not from Lema-dar, though I couldn't tell whether it was from Ton or another planet entirely.

They were poor, too. From their ragged clothes to their natural, un-augmented body shape. To their tribute, poorer even than in fairytales. Their guide mech was a simple thing and much outdated, though it had been oiled and polished very recently.

I felt sorry for them. I didn't want to feel sorry for them. I wanted to hate them.

In spite of their age, though, I doubted they had much experience on a rig. They had none of the confidence most would-be riders projected. 'Remind me who you crewed with?'

'Telphinus and Aba Mavus for one year,' they said. Their hands tightened on their cane.

They weren't experienced enough. Not by a long way. So why were they here?

'Why me?' I asked them.

They lifted their chin. Our eyes did not meet. Theirs were the dark brown of soil after rain. Mine, I knew, the amber of tree sap. 'You have experience,' they said. 'And I need someone I can trust.' Their thumb rubbed across the surface of the ancient coin repeatedly.

Unlike Boro, they didn't leave their tribute with me. It was a relief. I didn't want to keep that little piece of their heart, knowing I would have to break it. Unless this human was much more rig-experienced than they claimed (and I could think of no good reason to hide that), they could not be my equal partner.

As they left, I called, 'What was your name again?'

They stiffened, shoulders rising. Some in the crowd tittered, or spoke behind their hands with knowing looks.

I hadn't meant to humiliate them. I simply hadn't read their file.

But then, I was old enough to know that your own pain often leaked out into others in unexpected ways.

'Rin Loe,' they said over their shoulder. Then they returned to the line with the other waiting would-be riders, their head lowered.

The last human presented himself. A soft-looking man with a kind smile and well-made, plain clothes. He was perhaps fifty, with ash-blonde hair trending toward grey and dark, friendly eyes. 'I'm Jara Boon,' he said quickly, causing everyone to laugh, including a small chuckle from me, in spite of myself. 'Best to get that out of the way, just in case,' he said. 'I hope you'll consider me, Luxorian. I've flown with Talhara and Xenorius as rig crew, and in general believe in flying smart rather than fast, and avoiding scrapes where I can. I'm a good listener if you've a mind to chat, and I don't have the time to get angry or sullen when things go wrong.'

He offered me his tribute, a large blanket with a fine, tight-weave that would be very comfortable indeed. A worthy but not ostentatious offering, which I supposed was the sort of tribute I would have hoped for, if I had hoped for anything at all.

I dipped my head to him in formal acknowledgement, and told him I would consider him. As he returned to the line of would-be riders, I thought that if his file checked out, he would probably make a good partner. When Sar and I had chosen each other all those years ago, I would never have considered gentleness to be a necessity in a rider; afterall, what could a human hope to do to a dragon?

I had not yet been wise enough to understand that not all violence comes by way of a claw or fist.

It was a little while before the other dragons finished receiving their tribute. The two-headed dragon asked to deliberate further and contact the successful candidate later. The feathered wyrm who'd been so scathing of the offered humans warmly accepted a young woman who actually squealed in delight and bounced on the spot. A cheer went up, but I found it hard to share in their joy. I wondered if their partnership would work out well.

I wanted it to work out well.

But I also sort of hated their happiness.

I left the Tribute Fair as soon as I could, fleeing the market area with a careful haste. Much though I wanted to spread my wings and take off, I couldn't do so without sending a dozen humans flying and terrifying the rest. I felt not just the eyes of the humans and bots on me but also my fellow dragons. I shivered, fluffed up my feathers, and trotted faster down the street and out of sight.

I headed for Xax's, the only dragon-owned public house in Lema-dar, and one of only a handful built to fit a dragon's size that wasn't also open-air. I ducked through the wide double-doors and into the large hab-dome complex, laid out with enough room to shake out your wings without disturbing the other customers sitting at their little tables. The whole place had a surprisingly natural vibe; the ceiling had a trellis curving over it with vines twining along it and every table and booth, though made of old, dinged-up wood and metal, was surrounded by a bright array of potted plants. Ton as a planet was pretty green, but the region around Lema-dar was largely brushland. It was always nice to see some bright, leafy fronds instead of the patches of bramble and lone, brittle trees I had become accustomed to.

There were only two dragons in here now; one enjoying a large pot of drink and curled around a small table where two humans talked quietly, and the other behind the bar, directing a small bevy of humans and bots.

I made for the dragon behind the bar. She was a squarely-built drake, heavily scarred, largely scaled but with a long ridge of hair following her spine and topping her tail. Glittering blue scales and wings, but with silver fur.

'Hi Xax,' I said. 'Can I get a pot of lemly juice?'

Xax nodded and gestured to the human beside her wiping down the bar. They immediately left off their cleaning and set to work. 'Which table?'

'I'll take a booth in the back,' I said. There were a few dragon-sized booths that were good to curl up on and weren't sized to be human-friendly.

I headed there now, climbing onto the broad, padded seat and wrapping my tail around the base of the large table. It was a good size and a pleasant height; Xax had really done her work well.

I couldn't help but brood, watching the other dragons and their humans. The other customer looked like a Cosmic Defender, judging from the bright insignia on his padded vest, and the uniforms of the humans sitting with him. For all his job was violent and steeped in propaganda, he looked relaxed. Lazy, even. And at ease with these humans, presumably his rider and crewmate.

Xax was a different story entirely. She'd been a merchant dragon like me a long time ago, but had also done a bit of treasure hunting on the rim. Adventuring didn't usually pay well, but Xax had hit it big. She and her rider had both retired, and she'd made enough to start this pub and hire humans to handle all those small, fiddly things humans were so necessary for. She had no need of a rider anymore, though whenever her former partner came by, there was a big party at the pub.

I'd been a good enough merchant dragon but didn't really have a head for trade, or the kind of charm that could helpfully back up my rider. I'd thought Sar had more than enough charm for the both of us, anyway. But now I had no Sar, and the money I'd saved from the work was fast dwindling without picking up more. A few more months, and I'd be out hunting for my meals like a wild animal—and I'd have to leave Lema-dar, too, since the brushlands here couldn't sustain large game.

Two humans brought me a large pot of juice, which I lapped at sullenly. It was delicious: sweet and just a little bit sharp. Too pleasant for my miserable mood, because I wouldn't want to give up luxuries like this—but I'd been increasingly thinking that dragons had been wrong to ever leave the wild lifestyles of our ancestors. Yeah, maybe we'd only live to sixty, but at least we'd never have to make small-talk or ask a human to fasten a buckle for us.

A bot came into the pub, head turning in a perfectly level scan of the room. Its gaze fixed on me and it clanked toward me, servos and gears whirring with every movement.

I flicked the tip of my tail a few times to let out the nervous energy. What would a bot want with me?

'Excuse me,' said the bot. It had a humanoid but skeletal build, its face a blank mask but for the bulbs of its eyes and the slot for its speaker, where a mouth would be on a human. 'You are Luxorian?'

I inclined my head. 'And you?'

'I am Finder-X239. You may call me Finder.'

My ears perked forward, my interest piqued in spite of everything. Bots had never had much interest in me before. 'Hello, Finder. Can I help you?'

'I have looked at your file,' said Finder. 'I believe we could be of aid to each other. I am looking to do some materials retrieval for my colleague, Onna. I require a dragon and void rig, and can pay well.'

'Why a dragon and rig? Can't you just trade for what you need?'

Finder shook its head. 'We have very specific material needs which are not commercially or privately available. I must collect the samples myself, from remote planets, many on the rim.'

My ears flattened at that. There was something this bot wasn't saying. Most bots found lying uncomfortable—something we had in common—but unlike an autistic dragon, a bot could be perfectly comfortable lying by omission, or talking around the truth.

And some bots didn't have a problem with straight-up lying, either. The galaxy was a big place, after all.

'Alright,' I said. I started to drum my claws on the table, a rapid click that drew the bot's gaze. 'Why me?'

The bot stared at me. Unlike humans and dragons, most bots did not have mobile faces, and their thoughts could not be judged by facial expression. As I was not great at reading facial expressions anyway, I found this undaunting, though I read *something* into its momentary silence.

Maybe it was calculating another lie.

Or maybe I just made it uncomfortable. I was a fifteen feet-tall dragon to the shoulder. If you weren't a fifteen feet-tall dragon, I could see how that might give you pause.

'I have looked at your file,' said Finder. It left it at that.

'Well,' I said. 'I don't have a rig. I can't help you.'

'A rig can be provided,' said Finder. 'My partner and I would have no need of it when our material collection is complete. It would be reasonable to give it to you as an advance on your commission.'

An *advance* on my commission. An *advance*. A rig cost more than I had earned in ten years of flying trade routes. It had taken Sar nearly that long to pay hers off, even with a deposit paid for by her wealthy family.

With my own rig, I would have more freedom over my future than I'd ever had before. My fortune wouldn't be tied to my rider's.

But I would still *need* a rider. Or crew, at least. I couldn't maintain the rig, nor pilot it. I could only pull it. I shuffled my wings while Finder waited with the infinite patience of a bot.

'How much will you pay?' I asked.

'Two thousand credits for an estimated four weeks of work, with an additional ten credits a day per crew member for every day in excess to complete the task,' said Finder. While I was still reeling from that (and trying to keep my jaw from hitting the floor), it continued, 'And all board covered.'

There had to be a catch. There had to be. I wasn't Xax; I wasn't the one in a thousand dragons to discover an ancient treasure hoard. I was Lux, tired and left behind.

Perhaps Finder and its colleague already had a rig, and that was how they could afford this extravagance. Stolen it, perhaps, or rebuilt it from scrap. The rest of the pay was good, *really* good, but it wasn't void rig good.

But the rig...the rig offered me control of my own future.

'Would you supply the crew?'

Finder shook its head. 'I am not experienced enough to serve as crew, though I will assist with repairs and material extraction. It is my understanding that dragons and riders choose their crew together. I leave it in your paws.'

I looked down at my paws, still drumming, still restless. Always restless. Always in need of soothing.

Maybe it was time to actually do something.

'I accept your offer,' I said. 'I can have a crew ready in three weeks.'

'Two would be better,' said Finder. 'Do you have a com?'

I worked the small device free of the pack semi-obscured by my feathers. Even built to a more dragon-friendly size, I still found it awkwardly small and difficult to manage. Dragon paws were simply not mobile enough, particularly with our claws in the way.

Finder leaned forward and tapped its com to mine. I saw my screen light up with Finder's signal. 'Please remain in touch,' said Finder. 'If I may, I would like to be present for your hiring process.'

A catch. Just a small one. But with a sense that I was only seeing the first pebble of the avalanche, I replied steadily, 'Sure. I'll let you know.'

Chapter Two

When I got home, I had no choice but to look at the potential riders' files. If I was going to do this job for Finder, I needed a crew. And while I had no intention of partnering with a rider ever again, I had three potential rig crew who had already shown interest in flying with me.

I paced the small hab-dome I had called home for the last five years. It would be a mansion for a human, but for a dragon it wasn't much. A main room complete with an ostensibly dragon-friendly kitchen and a scrub-room at the back. In reality, I had enough room to curl up and to fill with clutter: piles of blankets; the thick balls of yarn I'd tried and failed to knit with my claws; various zines, both in audio transmitter and tablet form; small pieces of human art made with glass, crystal and metal. Bits of harness and packs were around too. It wasn't at all decorated; sometimes I dreamed of growing plants over the ceiling, like in Xax's pub, but I'd been too busy working as a merchant dragon with Sar, and then too depressed when she left.

She'd been dead against me getting this place. Lema-dar was a backwater, and buying a hab-dome was a huge extravagance. *'Why have a home somewhere I hate?'* she'd asked me. *'Afterall, we're a team.'*

I didn't want to think about Sar. I found a nice broad cushion and tangle of blankets to curl up in, placed my com on the small holo-dock that projected the screen to a size I could actually make out the details of, and started to go through the files from the Tribute Fair.

First, I looked at Jara's file. He'd made a good impression on me in spite of my bad mood. He'd seemed competent and kind, and I thought I'd quite like to fly with a crew of people who could coax a smile from me when I was stressed out.

He had over a decade of experience across multiple crews...he had paid off his own rig already with the money from his work...he'd been involved in hiring crews before...he had glowing references from *three* dragons he'd crewed with...

He had no reason to fly with me, except perhaps that he was older, like I was, and younger dragons tended to choose younger riders. That didn't mean I shouldn't contact him though. Surely it was worth trying?

I flagged his file and reluctantly considered Boro's. He had good experience and a glowing review from Verhalian and xer rider, Lis Tarven. They were the only crew he'd flown with, in spite of his long experience; the loyalty could be considered a plus by some, but I worried it would mean he'd expect the same from me, and I wasn't ready to offer it.

And then there was the fact that I hadn't liked him. I didn't have much time for people who got by on charm, and I had greatly disliked being flirted with by a human, of all things.

I looked at Rin Loe's file, but it was as expected. No rig, only a year of experience on a crew. I wasn't sure how they'd even gotten through the screening process to offer tribute. Perhaps they had a friend on the fair's committee; I couldn't imagine them bribing their way in, as poor as they'd looked. They had little to recommend them as a rider, especially to a more experienced dragon. But they might make good crew, with more experienced members around them.

I thought of their tribute, and the way they'd rubbed their thumb over the engraved surface. I liked them.

I thought about how much crew we were likely to need. Finder was willing to handle repairs, so it would technically be crew for the journey, but it wouldn't know how to run things. Then I'd need at least two more people; two to pilot, and ideally one more to handle maintenance. Crews typically ran between three and six people. I didn't want six if I could avoid it, but I couldn't trust a crew of three unless they were particularly experienced.

I'd aim to add three more people to the crew then. But before I contacted anyone, I wanted the advice of my mother.

I exited my hab-dome, the door sliding shut behind me. It was still bright out; thankfully, the Tribute Fair had been over with fairly early in the day, though I could still hear the distant sounds of bustle and merriness from here. My ear twitched irritably at the sound.

My mother, though, wouldn't be at the Tribute Fair. Wouldn't be anywhere in Lema-dar, or even on Ton at all. But I didn't like to com her from inside my hab-dome, so I shook out my wings, long green-and-pink feathers sliding over each other, and took to the air.

I loved the sky. Not the void sky a dragon like me was expected to pull a rig through. Just the open air of a planet, the ground falling away beneath my paws, the atmosphere a comfortable distance above.

Just because dragons were the only creatures that could fly the shining winds didn't mean that was where we most longed to be. The void was beautiful and dangerous. But a planet's sky was beautiful in its own way, and here I was the scariest thing around. A mighty beast, like in the old stories humans told of us, instead of the beast of burden so many of us had been reduced to.

Below, the spaceport town of Lema-dar shrank, becoming small and insignificant, full not of people struggling to survive but of tiny ants moving in trails and streams about their hill. I angled my wings to catch an updraft and shot up and away, leaving Lema-dar behind and, for a moment, my anxieties with it.

Brushland spread out below me, the mix of dry dirt and sand and short, brushy plants creating a speckled tapestry. The few sparse, leafless trees made for little more than scarecrows. I pumped my wings and soared higher, aiming for a distant cliffside where the roots of some long dead tree reached out like twisted fingers and nests of little birds were tucked among the rocks.

I landed on the largest shelf on the cliff-side, claws skittering on the stone, then turned and shuffled my wings. Though I'd landed near no nests, every bird in the nearby area took off in a cloud of shrieking feathers, as if I'd eat any of them raw, as if any of them could provide more than a taste to a being of my size.

I pulled my com from the small satchel strapped to my side. I held it awkwardly in my claws, rolling the wheel at the side until it found the name Tyroria.

I tapped her signal.

'Mum,' I said. 'You there?'

I stopped and waited.

A brief crackle, then: 'Luxorian, darling. How did the Tribute Fair go? Did you find a rider?'

I sighed. 'It went well enough. I'm thinking I don't need a rider, actually.'

A long pause. I could almost hear her working herself up indignantly, then calming herself down. Finally: 'Darling, we've been over this. You're a merchant dragon. You need a rider. Who is going to make the deals for you? Who is going to help care for you, and go where you can't?'

'I've been offered a job. Courier work, really. Materials retrieval and transport. It pays really well. I'd get my own rig. All I need is a crew.'

'But who is going to lead that crew?'

'I am. Mum...I led a crew before. Yeah, my rider helped, but–'

'Darling, you can't be inside the rig. You *need* a rider.'

I hated how she talked down to me like this. I was long since a grown dragon. I'd had a career as a merchant dragon for fifteen years. But to her, I would always be the late bloomer, her awkward hatchling compared to the siblings who'd flown the nest to great success.

'Well, I'm going to try this my way,' I said. 'Three people offered me tribute at the fair. I've already got my first crew member. I'm going to see if any of those three would settle for being my crew for a few weeks.'

'*Darling,*' my mother said, the sickly-sweetness of her tone turning forced. 'You can't expect people who are ready to become riders to sign up for yet another crew.'

'It's a short contract. And at least one of them is bound to say yes,' I said, thinking of Rin Loe. Rin needed more experience. Needed the work, like I did. 'But I don't want to insult anyone. Would you look at the files for me?'

'Me?' she sounded flattered. 'Well, alright, darling. You know I haven't flown a rig in a few years, of course.'

She'd actually retired not long after I started, but she was weird about her age so I let it pass.

Awkwardly, I sent her the files, nearly dropping my com in the process.

There was silence on the com for a little while. I settled more comfortably on my perch, curling my tail around myself and gazing out across the brushland. Lema-dar was little more than a twinkle in the distance.

Maybe there was a cave out here, like the wild dragons had used to live in. Maybe, if this courier job didn't work out, I could find such a cave and live off the land, hunting small game and drinking fresh water from the springs and gathering it from the rain.

Maybe I should do that anyway, and put this whole rig idea from my mind. At least then, I wouldn't be disappointed.

'I'm not so sure that any of these are going to be eager to join the crew of the dragon they expected to be equal partner to,' my mother said.

'No?' I dug my free claws into the dirt.

'No. But...I don't think there's any harm in trying. If you truly won't accept a rider right now, then at worst you're shunning winds you never intended to soar.'

'So I should invite them to my crew?'

'You should invite them to interview for your crew, unless you are very, very sure of them,' my mother said. 'You don't know any of these people. That's another thing a rider will give you that crew cannot: a rider will be living among the crew. Getting to know them. You'll be lacking your eyes and ears among them.'

'I have eyes and ears,' I said, lashing my tail.

'But yours cannot go where a human's could,' said my mother.

I understood what she was saying. Understood the gravity of it. Human crew I couldn't trust might steal from me, or steal my rig. They might make deals I didn't know about. A rider was a partner; it cut through all that.

Finder would be there, at least. It had a vested interest in our job succeeding, and it could go anywhere the humans would. Would live as part of the crew.

I tried not to think about the fact that I had no reason to trust it—or its too-good-to-be-true deal—either.

Chapter Three

'So what do you think?' I asked Rin. We were in Xax's, and I'd reluctantly given up my comfortable, dragon-sized booth to curl around a human-sized table and hopefully put the humans at ease—maybe even make them feel excited about having a dragon encircling them. I hated that I had to do that, that so much of my life seemed to be about making humans comfortable, keeping the humans happy—but I told myself that it was just for now. It wasn't like any of these people would be my rider; I wouldn't have to rely on them. Wouldn't have to be vulnerable with them.

I knew now that nothing good could come of that.

Rin threaded their fingers and frowned. They were wearing the same patched-up jacket as the previous day, and there were dark circles under their eyes. I wondered if they'd slept. Or eaten. Their mech paused and blinked a light at me. I wondered what data it was feeding its human about me.

I'd heard that guide mechs were as much pets as disability aids, having very basic intelligence and strong loyalty. They could only feed basic information to their humans, but could help with simple tasks. I'd not met one before and I was curious about it, but I didn't want to be rude.

'I applied to be your rider,' Rin said at last. 'Partners.'

I dipped my head in acknowledgement, but said nothing. I tried to keep my feathers from rising. I didn't want to give away my panic. If Rin Loe wouldn't accept my offer, how could I possibly convince the more experienced humans to join my crew? Two weeks was not enough time to assemble a good crew via public listing, not even in a spaceport town like Lema-dar.

If I couldn't get this job....

What?

Was I really going to run away and live like a wild dragon?

No. I'd have to go to Var-reel for their Tribute Fair at the end of the year, and I'd have to accept the best rider who offered me tribute there.

It was this or reliving Sar all over again, and I didn't think I could survive that.

'It's not personal,' I said. 'I'm not going to have a rider. You'll have as much status as anyone else in my crew.'

Their eyebrows rose. Humans had such expressive faces; it was good, because they were so small it'd be difficult to see otherwise. I thought maybe they were going to try to convince me otherwise—afterall, they'd wanted to be my rider. But then their eyebrows pinched together and they asked, 'Why don't you want a rider?'

I weighed my answer for a moment. 'I had a rider,' I said. 'It didn't end well.'

Rin breathed out hard through their nose, like they were cooling the fire in their pouch. 'I'll fly with you,' they said. 'Maybe I'll impress you enough to get a good reference for the next Tribute Fair.'

I nodded eagerly. 'Yeah. Yeah, of course.'

I thought back to their file. Only one year of experience in a rig. I wondered why they had decided to become a rider when they didn't even have a rig of their own yet. Why they had asked me, rather than a younger dragon that hadn't built up any wealth of their own yet, either. But that seemed like a pretty heavy conversation.

We tapped our coms to share signal. 'I'll be in touch,' I said.

Rin rose from their seat, then hesitated. 'Would...it be possible for me to sit in for your other interviews? There's someone else here, right?'

I looked at Finder, sitting silently on a chair to one side, not far from my outstretched forepaw.

I flicked the tip of my tail; the fan of feathers sent a faint breeze wafting across the table, stirring Rin's hair and coat. 'Why?'

Rin spread their hands. 'I might learn something.'

Though I knew they were inexperienced and aiming for rider status, something about the way they said it made me feel like they meant something more than simply learning the ins and outs of running a rig.

My reluctance must have been clear, because they added, 'I won't say anything. I just want to listen.'

My head swayed as I considered. It would be good to get Rin's trust early. To get all of the crew's trust. Without a rider to be my intermediary, the only person who could build a relationship with the crew...was me.

I'd always thought I'd had a good relationship with my crew. My last crew. They'd been kind and we laughed together sometimes. But I'd always felt a distance between us, too, that I hadn't known how to bridge. The distance of being a dragon and not being able to inhabit the same space, true, but also something else. I just...struggled to form connections with people. Maybe it was an autism thing, but I knew other autistic dragons and humans that had friends.

I'd only had Sar. And she'd been more than charming enough for the both of us.

But if it was just me...well. I was going to have to try.

Maybe Rin would be an ally in that, if I made them part of the process early.

'You can stay,' I said. I put a little warning in my voice. Rin didn't smile or cheer, they just nodded solemnly.

I turned to Finder. 'And are you happy with the process so far?'

Its eyebulbs flickered. I wondered if it was a bot expression I didn't understand. 'My happiness is irrelevant. It is fascinating and I would like to continue to observe.' It turned to Rin. 'I am Finder-X239. You may call me Finder. I, and my colleague Onna, are financing this rig and contract. I will be your crewmate for the duration. Let us shake hands.'

Finder held out its hand.

There was a pause, then: 'I don't like touching people,' said Rin. Were they hiding some anti-bot prejudice, or was that true?

Finder seemed unbothered. 'Of course. Let us wave instead.' It lifted its hand and executed a perfect wave, bending only the wrist.

Rin smiled and waved as well. Their obvious relief made me think they had been telling the truth. 'I'm Rin Loe. Nice to meet you.'

'I know you're Rin Loe, I was present for your interview. It's nice to meet you as well.'

I smiled and stretched, resettling in my position curled around the table. Something about that interaction, as stilted as it had been, set me at little more at ease. We all had to learn how to live with each other, but if they were all as awkward as I was, perhaps I'd make a good impression for once.

Rin's mech dragged a chair beside Finder's. I commed the next interviewee. 'Boro? Yeah, I'm ready for you.'

Boro swaggered in. His silver-streaked black beard and hair had been oiled, and he was wearing an outfit just as effortlessly wealthy as the last one—a long jacket that smelled of real leather, freshly-shined boots, and not a patch on his fine linen trousers or shirt. He reeked of some musky perfume or other. It smelled a little too much of prey animals to me.

He walked up to the table, spun his chair around, and sat on it backwards with legs spread to either side and his arms casually resting on the back. It looked...extremely uncomfortable.

What a truly bizarre little human.

'As I've already told you,' I said, 'I'm looking for crew for a fixed contract, maybe longer if we all get along. I have two crew members already.' I nodded down to Rin and Finder; Finder continued to stare at Boro, while Rin's head was angled down. Neither spoke. 'Pay is five hundred credits minimum for an estimated four week contract, plus ten credits per day over four weeks,' I said. 'All costs covered, and it'll be my rig we fly in, so you won't have to worry about repairs.'

Boro rested his cheek on his fist and stared at me for a few moments in silence. I hadn't the first clue what he was thinking. At length, he shifted and pouted his lips at me. 'This is a test, isn't it?'

I couldn't help but snort a puff of hot air. 'A test?'

Boro waved a leather-gloved hand toward Rin. 'I recognise them from the Tribute Fair. This is a test, isn't it? To see which of us will make the best rider?'

'It is not,' I said. I shifted my tail away from Boro, disliking having him within the curl of it. 'As I clearly stated when I extended this interview, I am looking for crew, not a rider.'

Boro said, 'But if I impress you—'

'Then I would be happy to keep you on, as crew,' I said firmly. 'Or send you on to the next Tribute Fair with my reference. This is a short-term crew contract, Boro. It's not even my contract.' I nodded toward Finder. 'Finder-X239 and its colleague are financing it. I am supplying the crew, that's all.'

Boro pouted his lips again. I flicked one ear backward, unimpressed. After a moment, he said, 'I accept.'

'Great,' I said. If he asked to watch my remaining interviews I was going to throw *everyone* out. But Boro only tapped his com to mine, winked, and strode out of the pub.

'Why do I feel like I'm going to regret that?' I muttered to the air.

Beside me, Rin snorted. I perked my ears at them questioningly, then said 'Mm?' when I realised they couldn't see that.

'It'll be fine,' they said. 'There are worse fates than an annoying crew.'

It was all too true.

The last interviewee was a complete unknown. When I'd called Jara, he'd respectfully declined. 'I'd love to be your partner,' he'd said. 'But the time's long past for me to become a rider myself. I thank you for thinking of me though.' He'd hesitated, then added, 'I know a lad eager for experience. No time on a crew yet, but handy enough, and a gentle sort. I'll send him your way.'

I commed the lad. 'Varek, I'm ready for you now.'

He entered with shoulders hunched high and a darting look around the room. A pale teen with neat, unpatched clothes and sturdy shoes. His hair was long and straight, nearly as pale as his skin.

I wasn't sure I could afford a less experienced crew member. Boro was plenty experienced, it was true, but Rin had only a year on a void rig and, as calm and possessed as they seemed, a year was a blink in rig-time. With Finder also inexperienced, taking on someone who'd never been on a rig before would be a risk. But Jara had recommended him, so I'd have to see how he handled himself now.

As soon as I had the thought, his eyes found mine. They widened, his mouth popped open, and I watched every muscle in his body tense.

This kid had never seen a dragon before. Or not up close, at least. He was going to pass out when he saw Xax behind the bar.

I held out a paw and waved him over. For a moment, I thought he was going to bolt back out of the pub, but then he hurried over and nearly fell into the seat. 'Luxorian?' he squeaked. Most human children were pretty squeaky, but this one seemed particularly so. I tried to gauge his age: sixteen? Seventeen? Less than half my own age, I was sure, though maybe fear was making him look younger.

He looked pretty sweaty, too. Slick. He stank of fear.

'You can call me Lux,' I said. I tried to say it gently, but to humans almost nothing we do looks gentle. 'Jara tells me you're a good lad. Reliable. What makes you think you'd make a good addition to my crew?'

He stared at me, jaw clenched. I realised his hands were gripping the sides of his chair so tightly that his knuckles had gone white. 'Hey. Varek.' I leaned my head forward, thinking to give him a reassuring bump, but I'd barely moved before Varek was up and out the door with a speed that made me think I'd underestimated humans.

'Well,' I said. 'That could have gone better.'

Finder said, 'Perhaps not. Varek appeared to be a human child, and additionally was terrified before he even noticed you.'

'People overcome fear, or work through it,' I said. I'd had to do it many times; I wouldn't have held it against him that he was scared, if he'd stuck around long enough to have a conversation.

I looked to Rin, who was chewing their lip. 'Rin. What do you think I did wrong?'

'Did you lean forward?,' they asked.

'Yes?'

They nodded, as if confirming to themself. 'That was probably it, then. Kid had probably never met a dragon before.' Their mech landed on their shoulder; they gave it a gentle stroke and it took off again.

'I was trying to comfort him,' I said.

Rin shrugged. 'Well. He probably thought you were trying to eat him.' They hesitated. 'Do you want me to track him down? Maybe I can convince him to come back?'

It was a surprising offer, and a kind one, but I shook my head. 'No, that's enough interviewing for today. Let's pack up, I guess.'

My tail twitched and I drummed my claws on the floor, over and over again. I was still down one crew member and had no other prospects to speak of.

Thirteen days to go. I was going to have to open this up more widely, and Sar had always said that public crew calls brought out the dregs of society.

I snorted hot air. I supposed I wasn't much better than the dregs anyway. At least, not to Sar.

Chapter Four

A dust storm hit on my way home. I didn't dare fly in it, but my feathers were fast stiff with sand, dirt, and grime as I fought my way through the streets of Lema-dar. All around, people were ducking into hab-domes or sheltering beneath roof shades. Two humans and a bot disappeared into a stack of crates and barrels outside a junk shop for the scant protection it provided. I wondered if bare skin and metal felt the sand more or less than I did as it tore at my feathers. I resisted the urge to spit sand out of my mouth: opening it would only make things worse.

A shadow passed overhead. I glanced up, expecting a ship, to see broad wings battling the wind.

'Hey!' I jumped forward, chasing the wyrm. 'Get down! LAND!' If the wyrm got caught in a blast, she could easily break a wing or worse. What kind of fool flew in a dust storm?

The wyrm didn't look back; she wasn't high up but the wind had likely snatched away my cries. I picked up the pace, buffeted by grit. 'Land! LAND!' Frustrated, I roared and flamed, showering myself in baked sand.

The wyrm's head turned toward the flash of light. She tucked her wings and dropped—or tried to, but the wind dragged at her wings. I rushed along below her, cursing the wind and the dragon, too, for flying in it. The dragon landed with a heavy thud and long skid, tail whipping as she turned to face me. I could barely make out her brown scales through the grime, and her large blue eyes were crusted with grit.

I shifted my wing to shield my face, careful not to open it enough to catch the wind. 'Shelter this way!' I said through a mouthful of sand.

The wyrm dipped her head.

We weren't far from home. I led her around the block to my hab-dome and stumbled, gasping, into the main room. She was quick to push in behind me, and we both audibly sighed our relief when the door slid shut behind her.

Dust and grit cascaded off me where I stood. It pooled on the floor and, every time I moved, it created several filthy waterfalls. I noted with choked despair that there was twice as much grime as there would have been if I hadn't chased down this foolish wyrm.

'I'm Syranos,' said the wyrm. She huddled near the door, large eyes taking in the utter lack of space in my hab-dome. We both fit in the main room but with barely a pretence of personal space.

'Luxorian,' I replied.

'Does it always storm like this?' she asked.

Ah. 'Not often, but too often all the same,' I said. 'Welcome to Lema-dar. It should blow over within the hour, probably sooner. Feel free to wait it out here.'

Syranos' ears perked, causing sand to run down her face. 'Thanks!'

I stared at her for a moment, hunched up like a cat in the wind and slowly shedding sand onto my floor, then shook my head. I headed into the scrub-room, trailing filth all the way. There, I found the enormous, rough-edged mirror to assess the damage.

I was not a particularly beautiful dragon, nor particularly vain, but this was unbearable. My green feathers, with their pink edges and iridescence, were all dull and brown. My curved claws and scaly, bird-like legs were similarly choked with dirt. And my long saurian muzzle had also browned. When I bared my long teeth, there was even dust in my *gums*.

I liked Lema-dar well enough, but there was nothing to like about dust storms. I liked dust baths as much as the next feathered dragon, but this was intolerable.

I eyed my shower cubicle sceptically. It was a squeeze at the best of times. Humans seemed to really resent the space we took up, and made everything for us as tiny as possible. Or maybe that was just being poor.

I wouldn't be able to stretch my wings, or likely scrub my tail. At best, I'd clog the drain and *still* be covered in filth but sludgy filth instead of sandy. I found showering deeply unpleasant anyway; a barrage of sensation while crammed into a claustrophobic capsule.

No. I'd have to wait out the storm to deal with this.

I reluctantly emerged back into the main room to be faced with a strange dragon and no idea what to say. Except for a desire to berate her for flying in a dust storm, but I had learned that berating people never went well.

I picked up the yarn just to give my paws something to do.

I never knew what to say to people. That had always been Sar's thing, and I had gladly left it to her. I wouldn't have been able to make it through the interviews if I hadn't long ago learned a good script for them. I had no script for 'a stranger covered in sand is trapped in your house'. It just didn't come up enough.

Syranos' ears perked. 'Does your rider live nearby?' she asked. Given a moment to take in the hab, she'd noticed the distinct lack of human presence. I didn't even have another room for a human to live in.

I didn't want to get into this. I hated the way other dragons treated me when they found out I didn't have a rider. Like I was pitiable...or deviant.

I wasn't a deviant. I was tired.

'No.' I left it at that.

One of Syranos' ears flicked back and the tip of her tail twitched, but she didn't push.

It wasn't long before the dust storm let up but awkwardness made the time stretch. When sand finally stopped buffeting the door, I untangled the yarn from my claws—I had achieved nothing, unable to concentrate in the presence of a stranger—and leapt to my paws.

'Storm's gone,' I said. 'Well. I'm going to fly to the river now to get this muck off me.' I congratulated myself on the excellent excuse to throw Syranos out. Sar had taught me how to signal things like that to people without directly asking them to leave, which was considered rude for reasons I was still fuzzy on.

'Oh!' said Syranos. 'I'll come with you. Where's the best spot to bathe?'

I held in a sigh. 'Head for the river, then follow me.' She wouldn't miss the river from the air. Lema-dar, like so many spaceports, had once been a port of a different kind. Though Lema-dar was far from the sparse ocean of Ton, it was the largest river in this part of the world, and canals criss-crossed it and travelled in all directions. Still used to this day for cheaper on-world shipping than void rigs or sky rigs could provide.

I emerged from my hab-dome, grit crunching beneath my claws. The city would have sand in every crevice until we got a good southerly wind. I took off in an explosion of dust and grit, covering the poor bot couple walking by.

'Sorry!' I called down as I climbed the air.

The city fell away and I made for the thick streak of blue snaking across the landscape, already running clear in the aftermath of the storm. Syranos bugled cheerfully and fell into the wake of my wings.

I landed in a clatter of claws on the rocky riverside with Syranos close behind. Another dragon bathed nearby, emerging in a thick shower of river-water. He was a furry drake and when he shook, his fur stood on end, turning him into a blue puffball. A human, likely his rider, attended him, laughing as he got drenched in the dragon's spray.

I dove into the water, my transparent second eyelids sliding across my eyes. The river was already running mostly clear in spite of the recently-passed storm; I could see the last trails of thickened silt rushing past and dissipating as they went. There were no fish nearby, but that was no surprise: prey animals were quick to scatter when a single dragon descended on them, let alone a trio.

I swam a bit, but my feathers were largely water-tight. I tried to puff them up, to deliberately let the water soak through to my skin. The drag of the water grew much stronger and I felt myself grow heavier, too. I emerged and clawed my way back up onto the bank, my feathers bedraggled, brown water pouring off me. I'd gotten the worst of the dirt off but I could still feel grit in-between my feathers, feel slime sticking my feathers to my skin.

Syranos emerged a moment later. 'Is it easier with feathers?' she asked. 'This stuff is absolutely glued to my scales, but I know feathered folk dust bathe.'

'I don't know whether it's better, but it's not great,' I said. 'I feel like my feathers are all coated in muck even though I soaked in the river.' I turned my head around and started preening my feathers, trying to nose them into the right positions, but it felt like I was just pushing the slime around.

Syranos trotted a little closer, still dripping water herself. 'Any tips for getting rid of it?'

'Grow hands?' I tried to flick the water from my tail. My feather tuft flopped like a wet mop. I would rather have dealt with the indignity without company.

'My home port is actually Gast, on Veth. We don't get desert storms.' She named a verdant ocean plant in our system. It was mostly floating islands, as I understood it, and Gast was like a travelling swamp with vines that moved when you weren't looking. I'd stopped there plenty myself.

33

'It's a bit arid here, but it's no desert. We only get them a few times a year, when the winds from the south are particularly strong.'

'I hate it,' Syranos said with bright cheer.

'Well. Same,' I said.

Syranos looked around and found a large rock and started to rub her side against it. 'This is humiliating,' she said. 'It's so much harder without humans.'

I studied her. She was probably only a little older than I was. If she had a home port on Veth and was travelling to Lema-dar, likely she was a merchant dragon or other traveller. 'You have a rider?' I asked her, trying to sound nonchalant. I had never met a riderless merchant dragon. It would be so encouraging to know that I wasn't trying to be the first.

'Oh, well, not *here*,' said Syranos. 'His husband's family are from Lema-dar, so we're visiting. And I thought it was a good day for a solo flight to take in the scenery.' She snorted and stuck her tongue out of one side of her mouth, a silly expression. 'You're right. I could really use some hands right now.'

Hands, I missed. Sar had been great at preening my feathers and washing off whatever gunk I'd gotten coated in on our travels. *It's kind of soothing,* she had told me. *I like helping preen you. It's time just for you and me.*

I swallowed down a hard lump at the thought.

'What about you?' asked Syranos.

'I haven't had a rider for a little while now,' I said, and it felt like the words had been ripped out of me. It was hard to be short with Syranos for long; she was just so *chatty*...

She ceased shaking out her leathery wings to stare at me. 'What, really? Do you work in town, or...?'

'I do contract work,' I said. 'I'm putting a crew together for my rig now, actually.'

'Wow.' Syranos flopped on the ground and rested her chin on her paws. 'I didn't know we could do the work without riders.'

There was no judgement in her tone. She was just impressed and maybe a touch confused. It was that earnest reaction that prompted me to say, 'Well...neither do I, really. I'll have to see how this contact works out, I guess.'

'I hope it does,' she said. 'I love my rider but...well...maybe we'll go our separate ways one day. Who knows?' She paused. 'Would you help me scrub my scales? I really don't want to go home with this stuff caked on. I'll help with your feathers?'

'Yes, thanks,' I said. Though I was often skittish of touch with strangers, this was a desperate situation. And there was something about Syranos' good cheer that had crept under my feathers.

When we finished, my feathers were neatly scrubbed and lying damp while I spread out on the riverside and sunned myself to dry them. Syranos dried faster than I did and said a cheerful farewell. I watched her go, wishing I'd had my com with me. It occurred to me that I'd never really had dragon friends. I'd grown up with my family, and with their riders, until I met Sar. If other dragons were as friendly as Syranos, perhaps I'd do well to try and kindle campfires there.

When I flew home and plopped down wearily in my nest of blankets, I got out my com and considered it. I still didn't have a full crew. I didn't think putting out a call for void rig crew was how I wanted to proceed, either. Just the three interviews I'd already held had badly drained my energy.

I needed a new strategy. Or maybe just a new perspective.

I scrolled to the right signal. 'Hey. Meet me at Xax's tomorrow at tri-night. It's time for our first meeting as a crew.'

Chapter Five

Xax's at night was not the same as Xax's during the day, which was why I never went. But Sar had always said that night's out with the crew were essential for bonding, and I needed to get a head start on that if I was going to ask for their help.

The door to Xax's slid open and I was immediately hit by a wall of noise and a wave of stench. A band had taken over one of the dragon-sized booths, using the table as a small stage. A musician blorted out a tune on some kind of long, reedy whistle, while another tortured an instrument with several strings and nozzles. The rest seemed to be attacking leather-skin box drums of various sizes, creating a loud, thumping pulse that went right through my bones and, weirdly, my bladder.

I knew dislike of human music wasn't common among dragons and Sar had often wanted me to pretend I liked it and humour her, but I just couldn't. My ears were so low they were practically plastered to my head and I still couldn't shut out the sound. The fact that they had taken over a dragon booth only added insult to injury.

The entire pub was choked with bodies, not just sitting at tables but standing around and talking. Some were even dancing, though thankfully that didn't seem to be catching on. I counted two dragons other than me and Xax; one laughing with some of their humans, another watching the band and tapping their tail along to the beat.

I wanted to set up in one of the dragon booths, but the only one available was far too near the cacophonous band for comfort. I made my way to one of the human tables. Large as I was, humans *had* to make room for me, but many of them were intoxicated, and the response was sluggish. Humans brushed against my flanks, some of them even reaching out to touch my feathers.

I shuddered, shrinking in on myself, but there was nothing I could do to meaningfully make myself smaller. I was a dragon among humans; I would never be small enough to go unnoticed among them.

I approached a near-empty human table. I didn't mean to scare anyone, but the human nursing his drink there took one look at me, immediately stood up, and disappeared into the crowd.

Well. Good enough. I settled around the table, wrapping my tail such that it fully enclosed it. My body would create some privacy for our group, much though I wished someone could offer me the same courtesy.

I rested my chin on my forepaws and waited. When I sighed, a gout of smoke burst from my nostrils, causing nearby humans to back away in alarm. After being touched by dozens of humans—some of them still touching me, brushing the feathers on my tail or back—I found it hard to care. I lashed my tail once, dislodging humans who had leaned against it and causing yet another stir.

I was a dragon, not some novelty statue. If they wouldn't respect my space, then I didn't have to respect theirs.

Or so I told myself. I remembered years ago, when I had rounded on someone who'd pulled a feather from my tail, snarling into her face, 'That *hurt!*'

And it had. I'd like to see how she'd have felt if someone had ripped out a chunk of her hair and left her scalp bleeding. But Sar had intervened with a placating smile and sent the human on her way. When I'd asked why she hadn't defended me or demanded my feather back, she'd gently scolded me. '*Humans are much smaller than you,*' she'd said. '*Using your size to intimidate them is being a bully, Lux. And I know you're not a bully, not really.*'

'But it was my feather,' I'd argued. *'What gave her the right to* hurt *me? How is it bullying to defend myself? I did nothing but complain!'*

'It's not the same, Lux. She's probably never even seen a dragon up close before. How would she know it wasn't okay?' Her disappointment had been so plain that my outrage had turned into confusion, then shame.

I'd been younger then. Looking back, I knew she'd been wrong to try to diminish me just to make humans more comfortable. But somehow, I still burned with remembered shame whenever I thought of it, mixed now with the new shame of backing down to Sar.

Finder was the first of my crew to arrive. I wondered, if I checked my com, if it would be early or perfectly on time. It walked as confidently through the crowds as it had through the near-empty pub on our last meeting.

I dipped my head in greeting. I tried to lift my ears to look friendly, but the noise was just too much and I soon had them flat again. 'Don't you mind the noise?' I asked them.

'WHAT?' Finder asked loudly.

Winds, but I could barely hear myself think in here. 'DON'T YOU MIND THE NOISE?'

'I TURNED MY AUDIO SENSORS DOWN,' Finder told me. Then they sat down at the table and looked around curiously at the pub-goers, looking utterly at peace.

I had never put much thought into the idea of audio sensors over ears, but they were looking *really* appealing right now.

I was also feeling the lack of a text com. They left it out of dragon-scale coms, since we didn't have the dexterity to type. I would much prefer to type than talk in this nightmarish environment.

Why had I invited everyone here again? Team-building? Advice? I was a fool.

Boro arrived next. He waved from across the room then danced his way over, frequently stopped by other humans as the crowd didn't part for him like it did for me. He got to the table, shouted, 'Anyone want a drink?' and disappeared into the crowd the moment I shook my head. He didn't wait for Finder's response, though I was sure there must be bot-safe intoxicants here, but Finder did not react as if it had heard him. I wondered if he would make it back to us or if he'd be snatched away by a crowd of fellow dancers.

Rin arrived last, stumbling out of the crowd. They looked like they'd been harried all the way across the floor, their hair awry, their expression murderous.

I shrank a little with shame. Even had I anticipated the crowds here, I wouldn't have thought about Rin navigating them without sight.

When I greeted them, they nodded curtly and touched their mech, which guided them to the seat beside Finder.

Finder's head spun around to look at them. 'ARE YOU WELL, RIN LOE?'

Rin's eyebrows shot up. They shrugged, then nodded.

Finder's eyebulbs flickered. 'THAT IS A CONFUSING RESPONSE.'

'It's a confusing question!' Rin said, but I was certain Finder couldn't hear them.

I lowered my head so it hovered over the table. Hopefully, I wouldn't have to shout to be heard. I curled my tail more tightly around the group, wistfully thinking that perhaps it would block *some* of the noise.

Winds, what did I *say* to them? Sar would be laughing, and buying drinks, and slapping everyone on the back. I didn't feel like laughing, Boro was buying the drinks, and if I slapped someone on the back they weren't getting up again.

'I wanted to discuss finding our final crew member,' I said.

'I CANNOT HEAR YOU, MY AUDIO SENSORS ARE TURNED DOWN,' said Finder.

Rin said something, lost in a sudden horn solo from the stage.

'I need help finding our final crew member!' I said more loudly.

'HELP WITH WHAT?' said Finder.

Rin rolled their eyes, stood up, and leaned forward so far that their face nearly bumped into Finder. 'Let's go outside!' they yelled.

'A WISE SUGGESTION,' said Finder.

Exhausted as I was, from both the sound and the conversation, I couldn't help but agree. I uncurled and stood up, my tail sweeping aside the various humans and bots that had been edging toward me. I ignored the hubbub and made my way out, refusing to cringe or shrink away from anyone this time. It was less out of sudden bravery than it was desperation to just *get outside.* Rin and Finder kept up in my wake, but neither of them crowded or touched me. That was a big relief; Sar had always insisted I allow the crew to touch me, to facilitate the feeling that I was 'their dragon'.

Maybe Rin and Finder just didn't feel like I was their dragon yet.

When the door slid shut behind us, I immediately collapsed onto my haunches and heaved an enormous sigh of relief that ruffled Rin's hair and coat.

Finder said, 'MY AUDIO—oh, sorry. My audio sensors have been restored to default settings.'

'Glad to hear it,' said Rin. 'Luxorian...what did you want to talk about?'

Right now? Nothing. I wanted to sit in blessed silence. I wanted to take off for the void. The void didn't have a drumbeat or sweaty humans or Finder yelling at me.

But we were on such a tight deadline to get this crew together, and what had I called this meeting for, if not to actually *talk* to my crew?

'This is...hard for me to ask,' I said. 'But do you have any recommendations for the crew, either of you? I can open public interviews but...I'd much prefer not to.'

I thought Rin might ask something accusatory, like why I, with my fifteen years of rig experience, couldn't call upon my own contacts. For most dragons, that would be nothing.

But all my contacts were tainted by Sar.

Rin tapped their lips thoughtfully. 'Recommendations? Not really. I wasn't particularly close with anyone on my last rig. But nobody was incompetent or anything. I can check if any of them are looking for work now. It's a good deal here, with an experienced dragon. I can't imagine anyone would turn it down.'

My ears perked hopefully—not so much from Rin's potential contacts, but from their assessment that this was a good deal. I wanted to ask, 'Even though I don't have a rider?' but I managed to restrain myself.

'I do not have any contacts within the void rig industry,' said Finder. 'Luxorian is the first contact I made, as the first dragon to fit the necessary requirements of the mission.'

My ears perked again at that, and Rin asked, 'What requirements?'

Finder said, 'As might be expected for a contract of this nature,' which definitely did not sound like an answer. Finder could be incredibly straight-forward when it chose to be, and right now, it was definitely choosing not to be.

I tried not to worry about it. I knew—I *knew*—that there was a catch to this contract. But if I got a rig, got paid, and came out of this with even a few crew members willing to stay on with a riderless dragon, then maybe I could have everything I wanted. That was worth it. It had to be worth it.

'Maybe Boro knows someone,' I said, unable to keep my ears from drooping. Boro was experienced and I was grateful he'd joined my crew, but I didn't trust his judgement. I had trusted Jara's, and that had failed spectacularly; how much worse would Boro's suggestions be?

'Where is Boro?' Rin asked.

I shrugged my wings. 'He said he was getting drinks.' That had been a while ago now.

Finder said, 'Unless circumstances were exceptional, Boro should have returned.'

'Maybe he met a friend or something,' said Rin, though they looked doubtful. I wondered whether they were thinking the same thing I was: that it was impossible to have a friendly conversation among all that racket.

I sighed and thumped my tail on the ground. I liked to thump my tail; there was something centring about it. I thumped it a few more times. Neither Rin nor Finder seemed bothered, which was reassuring. 'I suppose I'll have to go in and get him,' I said, my ears still flat.

'You don't sound like you want to go back in,' said Rin.

'I really, really don't.'

Rin scratched the back of their head. 'Well...I guess I can go grab him.' They didn't seem enthused by the idea.

Finder looked between me and Rin. 'You both find the environment inhospitable?'

Rin and I nodded.

'I will collect Boro. I can turn down my audio sensors.'

Rin said, 'It's pretty busy in there. Are you sure?'

Finder inclined its head. 'I am good at locating people.'

The auto-doors slid shut behind them, and then it was just me and Rin.

Rin plopped down to sit in the dirt, crossing their legs. I didn't often see humans sit on the open ground; they preferred to flutter around uncomfortably than get a bit of dirt on them. Or certainly, Sar had felt that way.

They petted their mech and asked, 'Why'd you plan to have a meeting here, now? I can't say I'm a fan of this kind of scene, and you clearly aren't either. We can't even hear each other in there.'

I hesitated, then dropped onto my belly, resting my head on my paws so that we could talk quietly.

'Bad advice, I guess,' I said. I studied Rin, expecting to see judgement or dislike, but they only seemed curious, in a mild sort of way. 'I thought it would be good for team-building,' I added. 'I've never put a crew together alone before.'

Rin leaned back, resting on their arms. 'Well, I think you're doing well enough, under difficult circumstances.'

'Am I?' I snorted. 'We're sitting in the dirt outside a pub right now.'

Rin shrugged. 'Could be worse. And choosing bad spots for crew meetings doesn't reflect badly on your leadership.'

I set one ear forward and one back. 'What do you think of my leadership so far, then?'

'Well...it's hard to say. But you're polite and you admit when you're wrong. Those are good places to start.'

I dug my claws into the dirt, then released the dirt. That...wasn't so bad.

Finder emerged. 'I HAVE LOC—oh. I apologise. I have located Boro. He is at the bar in discussion with another human. He did not heed my attempts to gain his attention, but it is possible he could not hear me.'

I sighed and stood up. 'Time to be crew leader,' I said. 'I'll be back soon.'

When the door sprang open, I was assailed by sound. I flattened my ears, lowered my head, and prepared to shove my way to Boro.

It turns out that if you move a little more forcefully, humans will hurry to get out of your way. Except for one human; I realised Rin was at my shoulder, the hood of their coat pulled up in a flimsy defence against the noise.

Xax wasn't at the bar, but as it had been sized for her to stand behind, it was a clear empty space in this miserable press of bodies. I could see over the heads of all the humans, so I could also clearly see

Boro there, shouting earnestly at the woman sitting beside him, who seemed a lot more interested in her drink.

'Boro!' I loomed over the pair. Not in a deliberately menacing way, but I was a dragon, and I couldn't help but loom over humans.

Boro spun on his seat. He had a bright blue cocktail in his hand and a slightly blurry expression. 'Luxorian! Look, this is who I was telling you about!' He gestured toward me with his drink, sloshing it on the floor.

The woman looked up from her drink. I saw she had some hex dice under her hand. She had hair dyed in flame-like colours of red, orange, and pink pulled into a messy tail, and she wore a practical dark grey boiler suit, the top tied around her waist, and a short-sleeved dark green top underneath. She was built along larger lines than Boro, tall and broad.

She considered me, not with awe, but with cool appraisal. No stranger to dragons, then.

'I'm Vala!' she said, without so much as glancing at Boro. 'Nice to meet you!' She nodded to me, as a dragon would.

I dipped my head in return. 'I'm gathering my crew for a meeting,' I said. 'I'm sorry to interrupt.'

'Don't be!' she flapped a hand and returned to her drink.

I perked my ears at Boro. 'Well? We're meeting outside, come on!'

Boro shook his head. 'Vala, is it?' he said. 'Vala...such a beautiful name!'

My ears flattened.

Rin leaned between me and Boro. 'Let's go!'

'But—!'

'Boss says we're having a meeting! Out!' They and their mech seized Boro's arm and dragged him away from the bar.

I hesitated then lowered my head closer to the woman. As before, she looked around with no alarm, just cool interest. 'Sorry about him,'

I said. 'I'm just putting my crew together now. He...wouldn't have been my first choice.'

'Don't worry about it,' she said. 'He's annoying, but harmless.'

I wasn't sure what to say to that, so I nodded and left.

Outside in the blessed quiet, Boro was pacing with his arms crossed, while Rin sat cross-legged in the dirt, and Finder stood sentinel, utterly still.

'Are we good to start?'

Rin nodded and Finder said, 'Yes.' Boro only grunted.

Well. So much for building goodwill with my crew.

'I don't want to keep you long,' I said. 'I'm looking for our last crew member. Boro, is there anyone you'd recommend?'

Boro stopped pacing, his surly expression vanishing. He looked delighted to be asked. 'Nobody as qualified as I, of course,' he said. He smoothed his beard. 'Hmm...Chera and Py might make good crew members, but I doubt either of them are in Lema-dar. I could reach out?'

'What's their experience?'

'Five years with Verhalian and Lis Tarven, plus whatever they've been doing the last year.'

'Verhalian let them go?' I said.

Boro shook his head. 'No, no...they just wanted to move on to other things. Good workers. Fun. Friendly.'

I suspected the latter statements might be more true. What's more, I wasn't sure I wanted to pad my crew with people indebted to Boro for getting them the job. Mutiny wasn't common, but it wasn't unheard of, and I already thought Boro was a little too entitled for my liking.

'Thanks, Boro. I'll bear them in mind.' I looked at Rin, and saw their lips were pursed and their brow knit. I wondered if they had been thinking the same thing I had.

I'd have to meet them, though, if either were available. I couldn't afford not to.

I dug my claws into the ground, grinding the grit between my claws. This wasn't good. I couldn't put together a crew I trusted on such a tight schedule, certainly not while also getting to know them and setting up a rhythm, An entirely new rhythm, since anyone with rig experience would have served with a rider.

'Luxorian? A word?'

My head turned. The door slid shut as someone entered Xax's, but beside it leaned flame-haired Vala, hands in the pockets of her boiler suit. I had no idea how long she'd been there; the door had been admitting and expelling humans in a near-constant stream. I'd like to think I'd have noticed her, but there was something very still and relaxed about her that defied attention.

'Uh...yeah, sure,' I said.

Vala jerked her head to the side and I followed her around the building, feeling the eyes of my crew on my back.

'You're looking for crew, right?' she said.

She'd been standing there for quite a while, it seemed. 'I am,' I admitted.

'And Boro isn't your rider?' She seemed more hesitant there than I'd yet seen her.

I snorted. 'I don't have a rider.'

She took that in for a moment. 'I don't have experience on a void rig,' she told me. 'But I'll not goggle at a dragon or scream at the first sign of a void horror. I'm a dab hand with a bolt gun, and I can fight with glass. And I know how to harness a dragon for solo flights.'

'And running the rig?' I asked, though it seemed foolish to be even entertaining this. A strange woman Boro had been pestering at the bar was not prime crew material.

She shrugged one shoulder, head swaying as she weighed her answer. 'I've spent a lot of time on sky rigs,' she said. 'Even did a fair bit of repair work on them. I hear the basics are not so different, but my main skills are in security and conflict management.' She paused. 'But

I learn quick and it makes no difference to me whether I'm taking my orders from a human or a dragon.'

I liked her. She was quick and to the point.

She had none of the experience I needed from our last member of the crew. I needed someone who knew void rigs in and out, someone level-headed and able to teach the others what needed to be done. Boro had the experience, but I didn't think he'd made a good impression on either Rin or Finder, and he'd made a bad impression on Vala.

I couldn't hire her. Boro couldn't be my most experienced crew member. He couldn't be my voice among the crew.

Did I need him to be? If I didn't want a rider, then surely *I* needed to be my voice among the crew. I would have to teach them, as best as I could. Though I'd never been inside a rig, I knew all about how they worked. Had listened to fifteen years of Sar's complaints and triumphs in running it, repairing it, and flying it.

'You might have to listen to Boro sometimes,' I told her. 'He's the most experienced member of my crew. But he'd be no higher ranked than you, and would have no right to order you around.'

Vala nodded slowly. 'That's fair. I can handle that. What's the pay?'

Wild that I had someone volunteering for my crew before even asking the pay. Either I was the luckiest dragon in Lema-dar, or there was some other catch here, like with Finder. Some reason Vala was desperate to sign-on with the first rig she came across, or perhaps needed to get off-world.

I studied her, trying to take my time with it, the way she had with me. Her boiler suit was stained in places with oil and generator fluid; she'd been repairing something as recently as today. She was younger than me, but not worryingly so; she was in her mid-twenties at least, maybe older, as she was wearing cosmetics.

She met and held my gaze. There was no challenge in her, only calm focus. She needed this, but she was neither going to beg for it nor fight for it.

'I have chronic fatigue,' she told me, answering the question I hadn't asked. 'It's hard to get security work when I might be too sick on a given day. Some days, I can't move at all. Somedays it feels like I can't *think*. But I manage it well, and I need to learn some new skills for when it gets worse. And I figure the work will be easier shared with a dragon.'

I looked down at my claws. I'd dug furrows in the ground while I thought. 'Pay's five hundred credits for four weeks, room and board covered, plus ten credits a day over. It's a contract job: materials collection on mostly unregistered planets. I can't promise I'll keep anyone on beyond that. We leave in two weeks' time.'

Her expression didn't so much as flicker as I listed the generous pay and conditions. I wondered if she even needed the credits; her clothes were so simple and practical, it was hard to judge her level of wealth, but they were undamaged and relatively new.

'Sounds good to me, Luxorian.'

'You can call me Lux,' I said.

She smiled. 'I will.'

Chapter Six

The next few weeks passed in a flurry of preparation. Finder showed me the rig, a large craft not dissimilar to the sky rigs I saw coming and going from Lema-dar. It was a compact, boxy thing of metal plates, as large as a human hab-dome—and rightly so, as a crew of humans and bot would be living in it. Not a particularly large rig, but plenty big enough for our crew. It had long wings that would open up like flower petals in the void. The tethers for it were made of wrapped metal wires, neat and well-made. It was a rather beaten-up rig but clearly well-maintained. Better than I'd expected, and I found myself worrying once again about the hidden catch in Finder's contract.

Strangest for me was the sense of ownership I instantly felt. I wouldn't live in this rig with my crew, but it was mine. My livelihood, my autonomy. I got a large cloth and some polish and set to cleaning it while the crew went in and out. Finder didn't reveal that the rig was part of my payment for the contract, which I was grateful for. Though a rider and dragon were entitled to a larger share of a rig's profits, an entire rig was an incredible extravagance.

I ferried food rations and basic living supplies to the rig, avoiding the worst of the traffic by air. Meanwhile, the crew familiarised themselves with the controls, the repairs, and the general function of the rig. Boro and Rin explained to Finder and Vala while I listened and cleaned the rig from outside, their voices carrying through the open door. In flight, I'd be able to com the rig when necessary, but I'd never be in there with them. Rin was more knowledgeable than I'd have guessed from their experience, and they spoke with confidence. Boro had become a lot meeker since Vala joined (though he'd begged me not to hire her when I first told him), and it seemed like peace was entirely possible with my crew. We ran the maps, plotted our trajectory, and in general put a plan in place.

So when the time finally came to set off, Boro ran the crew through the last-minute launch checklist, and we were ready to go.

I flexed my wings and shifted from paw to paw, feeling the shape of the harness around me. A void rig harness was nothing like one you might yoke a beast to plough a field; it was sophisticated tech encasing my chest, head, and sides in armour, and a long, flexible cascade of tethers connecting me to the rig itself, so that I could pull it. It fit nicely, if not perfectly; it had none of the worn-in-ness of my old harness in Sar's rig. Which now some other dragon wore, no doubt.

I didn't want to think about Sar today.

Unlike a human, I didn't need an air-tight suit and helmet, so my harness was more reminiscent of the ancient armour of dragon-mounts of old, though significantly more high-tech. An open-faced helmet with visor screen and room for my ears to emerge and a wide-fitted chest-plate being the bulk of it.

In my ear, I heard Rin say, 'Checks complete, flight-ready.'

'Flight-ready,' I replied. And then, filled with a sudden burst of excitement, I snapped my wings out and cried, 'Let's go!'

I leapt into the air just as Rin hit the boosters on the rig. But the boosters were only to ease the lift off—no force in the world could keep up with a void-bound dragon.

I pumped my wings and felt not just air currents but the threads of the shining winds. Weaker planet-side, but ever-present. I felt my entire body fill with electric sparks; my feathers glowed, lit by the shining winds that were intangible to all other creatures. I shot upward, my speed such that I was dragging the rig after me even as it burned its thrusters at full-power. A rig could make it into space, but it couldn't travel through the void faster than light could. Distance was trivial when you flew the shining winds. When I pumped my wings, the ground vanished. Twice, and the planet was an orb hanging in the void. I glided a moment; in the void, the shining winds were stronger, carried me more actively. I could see them travelling in all directions, shimmering pink threads of current that encircled planets and travelled deep into space.

'We've breached void,' said Boro in my ear. 'We're prepped to soar.'

My muscles tensed. I angled my wings. 'Ready. Go!' I beat my wings three times in quick succession, filling again with electricity and light. My flight feathers flashed and we were travelling only the winds, the void giving way to the winds which surrounded us like a river of pink light pulsing with lightning. I had asked Sar what it looked like to her when I soared, and she had said inky darkness, a void without stars or planets. Humans had so much, but the shining winds were only for dragons. A beautiful loneliness.

'Are we stable?' I asked Rin on com. I had a device embedded in my harness. It took only a few presses to tap a signal from the rig.

'We're stable,' said Rin. 'That was a fast ascent. Smooth, though.'

I flicked my ears. 'I've been doing this a long time.'

'Experience doesn't make it less impressive,' said Rin.

'Is everyone okay in there?' I asked. I had no way to see inside the ship.

'Vala's comforting Finder. It's not its first time soaring, but it doesn't like it. Boro wants to crack some alcohol to celebrate our inaugral soar, but we shut that down pretty fast.'

'Thanks. Out.' I tapped Finder, who opened its com. Unlike humans and dragons, bots didn't need external devices for long-range com or data. 'How're you holding up?' I asked it.

'I am structurally sound,' said Finder. I thought there was a hum in its voice I'd never heard before, but perhaps that was just its com.

'I've done this countless times,' I said. 'We're safe.'

'Statistically, soaring is never safe,' said Finder. 'Any number of malfunctions could occur to the rig, causing us to fall out of the winds. Steering errors from you could do the same. And then there are the horrors.'

I took in the winds around us, serene and uninterrupted. 'No horrors here,' I said. 'But if there were, I'd drop us out of the winds. They don't track well when you stop soaring.'

'You wouldn't fight them?' Finder asked.

'I could, but I wouldn't,' I said. 'That's an unnecessary risk.'

The horrors. Enormous shadow creatures that preyed on those deep in the void, and which could sense us even as we soared through the shining winds. Larger than a dragon, though not more dangerous than us. There weren't so many around inhabited systems now; the Cosmic Defenders, much though I disliked them, had killed or driven off all but the sneakiest horrors over the last hundred years. But in the outer wilds of space, they were much more plentiful.

I wasn't so worried for myself. A horror would have to be unbelievably vast to pose a lethal threat to a dragon of my age, as I was both experienced and fast. But my crew, and my rig, were vulnerable if I couldn't drive one off fast enough.

And that was why I practised avoidance. I knew some dragons saw it as our duty to fight horrors where we saw them, but I had never subscribed to that. My first duty was to the safety of my crew, and I didn't style myself as a hero. Heroics wouldn't serve them.

Finder said, 'I am updating my risk models. This is still a terrifying endeavour, but less so. Thank you.'

'No problem. If you're worried about anything else, let me know.'

There was a pause, then, 'I am worried about a great number of things, but I will bring any pressing anxieties to your attention.'

They tapped out, leaving me to my flight for a while.

It was a normal part of soaring, the isolation. Though my crew were all behind me, though I was hooked up to their rig by huge collection of wire tethers, I was removed from them by experience. The rig I couldn't see or hear into, the winds they could not perceive. Unless something was wrong, I was unlikely to hear from them again. And while I enjoyed soaring, in its way, that couldn't help but feel lonely.

I beat my wings again, feeling the winds ruffle my feathers with its strange, static charge. I was told technology could not detect the shining winds, that for most creatures the void was utterly still. I had often wondered whether any dragons had been involved in the making of that technology, because for us the winds were trivial to detect.

As I flew, I kept a wary eye on the edges of the current, through which horrors could sometimes be seen. All the warning a dragon might get was a faint shadow against the light before some vast beast made entirely of teeth, or eyeballs, or tentacles, or teeth, eyeballs *and* tentacles, would lash out and try to eat your rig.

Maybe it was better that we dragons soared alone then, with nothing to think of but the winds and the horrors.

Someone tapped my com. 'Lux?' It was Rin.

'Yeah. Is everything all right?' The idea that something could have gone wrong so quickly did cause my pulse to pick up a bit. I needed this contract to work out.

'Yeah, yeah. Everyone's settling down now for the journey. Vala is teaching Finder some kind of dice game. Boro sounds like he's asleep, honestly. Vala says he's curled up on a chair under a flowery crochet blanket.'

It was a nice image, a cosy crew scene. Not the disaster I'd been expecting when Rin tapped.

'Have you ever been to uninhabited planets?' asked Rin. 'Hazanthis is pretty far away from any of the paths I travelled when I crewed with Istharoon. I mean, obviously we all know what to expect; hostile wildlife, dangerous chemicals, and all that. But I guess I'm just wondering what it's like to set foot on a planet you know hardly anyone has before.'

I considered. 'I've been to two uninhabited planets on the rim before, though several low-habitation planets. The one that sticks out to me was the first planet, Por. It was an ocean planet and an odd contract for us; we were a merchant crew, and tended to stick to our trade routes, but we'd been offered a vast pile of credits to make a supply run there to the little five-human crew surveying it.'

Rin made a little interested sound, prompting me to go on.

My eyes scanned the winds around us. 'We had to make an ocean landing; there were a few islands about but the surveyors had set up underwater. I detached from the rig and it went down; dragons can swim, and we can breathe the winds when air is lacking, but we don't have the same speed or agility underwater that a rig can. So they dove and I tucked my wings and floated on the surface. Did my best not to get swept away by the current, but I had my com if it came to it. And it was beautiful there. Something about the atmosphere turned the sky purple, and the water reflected that. The waves were very gentle. There were four-winged creatures flying in the air—insect-like, I guess, with jewelled wings. Like dragonflies, but about the size of cats. They seemed curious about me, but I flamed the air once and they darted back to give me space.

'It was...I don't know, I can't express it. Being in the wilderness on a populated planet, no matter how far away you travel, feels different. It's frightening, but also magical. I nearly choked on my own gizzard when I saw a vast, insect-like whale breach the surface of the ocean, but watching its glittering body cycle back down into the waters is also a sight that will always stay with me.'

Rin cleared their throat. 'Did you get attacked?'

'My crew did. Something in the deep saw the shiny metal and thought maybe it was lunch. That's always an issue when a crew sets off without their dragon, because very little mistakes *us* for lunch. They made it out okay, though.'

'Did it bother you, being left behind?'

I weighed my answer. I had been upset when I found out what had happened. Sar had turned it around on me. *'If you were so worried something might happen, you should have pushed harder to come!'*

'Yes and no,' I said now. 'I wish I'd been there to help them. And it gets lonely sometimes, being left behind. There are so many places dragons can't or aren't welcome to go. But I did love the quiet time I spent floating on the surface of Por's ocean.'

'Well...I guess you're the boss now,' said Rin. 'You get to decide whether you stay behind or not.'

If only that was true.

We talked on. Rin shared some of their experiences from their year on a rig; I told them about some of my favourite crew members from mine, carefully talking around my former rider. Some of the other crew members joined the com, too, when they realised Rin was chatting with me. Vala asked me if I liked games of chance; Finder explained that there was an optimal decision to be made in any game involving probability; Boro told me how vigilant a crew member he was being, his voice still heavy with tiredness from his nap.

I saw no shadows beyond the shining winds, and no horrors leapt out to munch on my rig. I don't know at what point it happened, but my crew left their coms open, so I could hear everything going on and join in if I chose.

I thought of my first breathless soar with my first rig, excitedly waiting for Sar to contact me. How I glowed and puffed up at her praise.

This was better. This was so much better.

Maybe I was going to pull off this whole riderless rig-dragon thing after all.

《 》

'We're approaching Hazanthis,' said Boro.

'Got it. I'm dropping.' I slowed my flight, then caught myself in the shining winds, wings pumping backwards. As I did, the system around me slowly came into focus. We were a safe distance from any planets, and I couldn't see any horrors. I glided out of the shining winds' path and out into open space.

It was always jarring, when you stopped soaring. Everything that had been the beautiful current-like lights of the winds was suddenly both busy and empty. Planets and stars burst into life, bright among the dark. And all around, the void. I could still see the threads of the winds, but as I stopped trying to fly them they faded from focus, faint in my awareness.

I looked around, my motions weightless in the void, my feathers floating askew. Without the winds, the void was a very different place. Airless and quiet. I took in the planets nearest us.

'That's Hazanthis,' said Vala. 'Yellow. Dust planet.' I found it among the planets hanging in the void. It had been a well-timed drop; Boro really was experienced. I flapped my wings, catching just enough wind to give us direction. I didn't bother alerting the rig; if I wasn't soaring from planetside, they had no reason to burn to keep up. I'd pull them along just fine.

Hazanthis loomed larger and larger, swelling before me. Going from an orb to something too vast to fully see. I tucked my wings for entry.

We plummeted at incredible speed. 'Brake!' I called on com, and snapped my wings out. The rig slowed with me as the clouds parted and we glided out across a vast world of yellow rocks and dust. There was some water here, lakes, rivers, and even distant oceans, but it was overwhelmingly rocky. As we glided, I scanned around; I didn't see any megafauna, though my eyes were keyed to movement and I could make out some small skittering somethings against the rocks.

'How's the surface integrity?' I asked my crew.

'I'm on it,' said Vala. 'Deploying scout.' I heard but didn't see the little drone click free of the rig and zip down to the surface. I turned my flight into a circle, pulling the rig after me; our drone was good quality, but it couldn't keep up with me, and I didn't want to lose it on its first outing.

Below us was a fractured plateau of rock, the crevices potentially running deep, but too narrow for me to really tell. I thought the skittering things might be lizard-like, though flatter, like discs. Their camouflage definitely suggested there was some larger predator about, though anything that preyed on something so small was unlikely to be a threat either to me or to my crew.

'Surface integrity is 93%,' said Vala. 'That's good enough for me, but it's not without risk.'

'You get out first,' I said to Vala.

'From the air?' It sounded like a genuine question. I hadn't known humans could safely deploy from the rig when it was airborne, but her confidence told me they could and she had.

'No, land the rig, then you get out. I'll take off and look for predators big enough to threaten you. But if I follow you on the ground, we'll never find out. Nothing will approach.'

'I like that plan.'

I thought about what would keep my crew safest. 'Rin, Boro, stay ready to sky launch. Wait for Vala or my signal. Don't launch without Vala." The rig, while not powerful enough to fly the void at a useful speed, was just as mobile as any sky rig. They'd be able to take off.

'Yes, boss,' said Rin. It would have made me smile to hear it, if my mind wasn't entirely on the problem in front of us.

Ultimately, it would be my crew that would find Finder's materials. I had neither the technology nor the capacity to operate it. But as their dragon, their safety was up to *me*.

I touched my harness chestplate, manually releasing the many wires and cables connected to it, but I left my harness on, lest I needed to reconnect in a hurry. Unless we'd landed in civilization, it didn't make sense to take off my kit. The rig whirred as it reeled in the tethers, keeping them safe.

I flapped forward, trying out my new weight-balance. It was always an adjustment when I first freed myself, but it only took a few seconds to get my bearings. Meanwhile, the rig made a slow, gentle landing, folding its petal-like wings and kicking up a vast ring of dust around it. After a moment, the door unhinged into a ramp and Vala strode out, a bolt-gun in her hands and a long glass blade strapped to each hip.

Though I'd seen a fair few glass knives—the sharpest and deadliest weapons, and thin enough to be easily concealed when needed—I hadn't ever seen a glass sword. I knew they were still around, but with the prevalence of bolt-guns and other projectiles they'd lost a lot of their popularity. I'd imagined them a relic of the time of ancient dragon-riders, which was probably why they appeared most often among Cosmic Defenders, even if only ceremonially.

Vala looked like a modern knight herself, striding out with both caution and confidence. She wore an armoured hab-suit with plating on the chest, head and limbs, the glass face of the helmet opaque. Though we knew the planet was non-toxic and the air was safe to breathe, Vala was first out and might get jumped by an angry predator or parasite. She'd be glad of the protection, then.

I circled above, still scanning for threats. There were some large, slow-moving creatures beyond the river, walking in a long trail. From the way they clumped together when my shadow passed over them, they were likely prey animals, and there was likely an aerial predator large enough to cause them some concern.

I tapped Vala's coms, and made sure to forward it to the whole crew. 'I think there may be large or dangerous animals in the air out here.'

'Large and dangerous like you?' Vala asked. I noticed she didn't look up; she trusted me to cover above, even though we'd only just met. It struck me again how comfortable she was with dragons. Not just comfortable, but aware of how we worked. She must have some history with a dragon, or with multiple dragons. Perhaps, once we knew each other a bit better, she'd share it with me.

'Probably not large and dangerous *to* me,' I said. There weren't many creatures like dragons in the galaxy. We could even fight much larger creatures simply because we were sentient—that was why void horrors were not particularly horrific to dragons.

'But possibly large and dangerous to us squishy little mammals,' said Vala. 'Got it. Thanks.'

But while I flew a widening spiral, I never saw anything in the sky or on the ground to give cause for fear, and Vala encountered nothing but the disc-lizards and some small, furred creatures that vanished in between the cracks on approach. I sent Vala back to the ship to escort the rest of the crew off the rig.

Finder, for all its anxiety in the void, was singularly focused once it set foot on Hazanthis. It had a variety of survey equipment and sent our two drones off to search as well. I landed, sending a wave of dust (and complaints) over rig and crew, but Finder never so much as paused as it considered its small computer and started analysing the data both from the dust it had gathered and from the drones drilling and collecting in various locations nearby.

While Finder worked and Vala stood guard, Rin and Boro went over the rig, doing the early-prep work necessary for launch as well as checking the hull for damage. Sometimes, on entry, a rig could sustain damage from superheated particles in the atmosphere. It was rarely threatening to a safe launch or further travel, but it was good practice to get it patched up.

With everyone so busy, I felt at a loose end. Just my presence here would deter most threats, and I couldn't fly further afield and assist in Finder's search without leaving my crew at risk.

'Is there anything I can help with?' I asked Finder.

Finder looked up from where it had been staring into the distance while it processed the data from its drones, the computer holo-screen utterly irrelevant to it. 'Scout Two has detected a potential vibroxis deposit in a large cave. If you could ascertain that the cave is safe for the crew, that would be helpful. If it is, we can set up there and begin extraction.'

I used my com to ping Scout Two and it pinged back. It wasn't far away, but I still didn't like to leave my rig and crew undefended.

But it wouldn't necessarily be undefended. 'Vala?' I turned to my security specialist.

She was hard to read in her armoured hab-suit. 'I can handle it,' she said. 'The area here is clear, but if something did jump us I believe I could hold things together long enough for you to get back to us. And I certainly can't make the journey as fast as you can.'

It was true. And if this contract was going to work out, I'd need to learn to trust my crew when I wasn't watching them. Not just trust them with my rig, but trust their judgement. If Vala thought she could handle it...

'I'll be back soon. Com if you need me.'

'Got it, boss,' said Vala.

I strode away from the rig, took two big leaps, and then swept my wings down to carry me into the air. I pinged Scout Two again—it's signal was coming from a small cave embedded in the edge of the plateau. Below was just more dust and rock; this part of the planet, at least, was not terribly varied.

I glided over the edge of the plateau and then circled back around. It looked like my crew would be able to make their way down to it by foot and it would only be a little treacherous. As I tucked my wings slightly to land in the cave, Finder tapped my com. 'Scout Two detects large organic life in the nearby vicinity.'

A breath later, Rin tapped in. 'There's a bear or something near Scout Two. Be wary.'

'Thanks,' I said to both, and ended the com. I didn't want them to worry if they heard me snarling.

I landed with a slight skid, my claws sliding on the dusty shelf as I ducked into the cave. It was high-ceilinged enough that I could stand at my full height, but the entrance was a little narrower. My tail lashed as I found my balance. It was dark, but not worryingly so; most dragons need very little light to see, as our eyes are ultra-reflective.

The inside of the cave was...a lot like outside the cave. Just dusty yellow rock, but minus the sky. It looked like there was a large tunnel leading down however, so I pinged the scout and it cheerfully pinged back and I thought...well, I can't say I've cleared this yet. I threw a cautious glance over my shoulder in case the not-bear was about to pounce on my tail, and then I made my way deeper into the cave.

It was much larger than I'd anticipated. The tunnel plummeted but the ceiling remained high. And I smelled...life. A whole lot of life. Vegetation. And there seemed to be a rising glow ahead.

The tunnel opened out into a lush cavern with hanging vines, running water, and a carpet of thick, luminous moss. The scout perched on a rock, probe buried in it. I looked around; there were lots of creatures here. Disc-lizards, like I'd seen on the surface, but also bright slimy blobs in all colours, no bigger than the tip of my claw or the span of a human palm, on whom I could barely make out the features of head, tail, legs, and tiny, translucent feet. Odd, blobby amphibians.

They didn't seem disturbed by the enormous dragon in their midst. I leaned down to sniff the nearest one that sat, wobbling, on a knot of moss. It didn't smell particularly toxic, but I'd advise the humans not to touch them until we were sure. It didn't so much as twitch at the nearness of my relatively enormous maw beside its tiny body. This close, I could see that its eyes were simple black sensor dots, its mouth little more than a slit in its blobby head. Perhaps it wasn't sophisticated enough to be afraid, or perhaps being eaten was part of their species' survival strategy. There were certainly a lot of them.

I tapped Vala's com. 'I think it's clear here. No sign of the large creature. I must've scared—FUCKING WINDS!' I roared and twisted back on myself; there was an enormous cat on my back.

Chapter Seven

The cat-thing had like a dozen legs and all of them were tearing into my feathers while it chomped on one of my wings. I tried to buck it but it dug its claws in harder. I snarled at it. 'Get OFF!'

'You got this, boss?'

'I'll com you back!' I growled, and tapped out. The cat-thing got a hunk of wing in its mouth. 'Ouch!' I snapped my wing out, dragging it off my back; each of its claws came free with a clump of bloody feathers. 'You awful, sneaky little fucker!' I flapped my wing and it swung around like a ragdoll, jaws still locked on my wing. I felt my flame rising, ready to torch this thing and be done with it. I could taste sulphur as smoke poured out of my mouth. Then I choked it back; I couldn't flame in here without burning up this entire ecosystem, including the hapless little blobs.

I couldn't twist around enough to get the thing in my claws and prise it off, but my neck could reach that far. I seized it between my jaws; it shrieked and let go of my wing as my teeth bit into its tiny, feeble, cat-centipede-thing body.

'Bad kitty!' I said. Well, what I actually said was, 'Bmph-mphy!' but since it couldn't understand me anyway, I doubted it mattered. It tasted awful: blood like hot oil, and its fur was filthy. It struggled in my grip but in a wild way; it couldn't bring any of its many claws to bear. I could tell from its panic that it thought it was about to die.

Winds, I hated killing things. And it was only some stupid cat-thing. Dragons the galaxy over have a soft-spot for cats. I carried it back out of the lush cave and onto the cliffside.

'Bmph-mphy!' I said again, and tossed it onto a lower shelf of the cliff. It shrieked again, sounding like nothing so much as claws on a rusty metal sheet, and scrambled away, disappearing behind some rocks. Not trailing much blood, so I hadn't hit anything vital. I hoped I hadn't, anyway. 'And stay away!' I said for the sake of my crew, puffing up my feathers so I looked even bigger.

Well. As many feathers as the cat-thing had left me. I studied my back; no properly bald patches, but definitely some clumps missing. And a hunk out of my wing, and *so* much blood. Feathered dragons bleed more than furred or scaled dragons. It's just a feather thing; they hurt like hell when they get ripped out, and frankly they are *too easy* to rip out.

Once I was done mourning my feathers, I got a hit of powerful oil-aftertaste from the cat-thing's blood. I gagged.

Vala tapped my com. 'All good?'

'All good. Give me a moment to check the cave's clear. Have Boro bring the rig over.' I paused. 'And pour some water for me. I need to swill out my mouth.'

《 》

I trod air outside the cavemouth while my crew made their way down the rocky cliffside path. Rin and Boro were both wearing hab-suits even though the air was breathable; unarmoured hab-suits provide a little extra protection, and the in-built coms could project onto the helmet screens, so I supposed it made sense.

It always made me nervous, humanoids in high-up places. And I was extra worried about Rin. It was a precarious place for their mech to guide them through. They had their cane out, feeling the path ahead.

Boro and Vala sandwiched them. The humans all pressed sensibly close to the cliff-face and tested each step, but even so I stayed on high-alert.

Once the last of them—Finder, in this case—made it in, I tucked my wings and landed next to them with a thump and a skitter. My tail knocked into Finder, who stumbled but didn't complain.

'Oh. Sorry.'

Finder's eyebulbs flickered.

'Scout's deeper in,' I said. 'There's a lot of little creatures in there. They aren't shy and they might be toxic, so don't touch anything with bare skin. Or metal.'

'Yes, boss.' I thought Vala's voice might've sounded a bit wry.

I let Vala lead the way and bookended the group. Rin walked just ahead of me, their cane tick-tocking from side to side. 'Didn't trust us to make it down the cliffside ourselves?' they asked lightly. 'I could hear you.'

'What? I didn't—' I stopped, thinking of how I'd hovered nearby. 'A dragon is responsible for their crew's safety,' I said. 'And you don't have wings and you have stubby, clawless hands.'

'So...no,' said Rin. It sounded like they might be holding in a laugh.

I grumbled a bit and said, 'You'd have been pretty grateful if you'd slipped.'

'I would've. I'm grateful now. It's good that you care about us.' They paused, then added, 'You're so anti-rider, I'd thought that maybe—?'

'That I hate all humans? That I'd delight in letting you fall to your deaths?' I snorted, a little hotter than intended, and smoke curled around Rin as they walked. 'Why are humans like this? What is so wrong with me wanting to be accountable only to myself?'

'I—I'm sorry.' I couldn't see Rin's face with their back to me, not that I had a great track-record of interpreting facial expressions. 'That was a stupid thing to say, and it's not really how I meant it. You've been a good boss, and friendly, too. I guess I hadn't thought you'd want to talk to us, laugh with us. The last dragon I crewed with didn't have much to do with us and left it all to his rider.'

I digested this. Their words still got under my feathers, but I could understand them expecting me to be aloof, all things considered. I'd been aloof to my former crew, even if not by choice. 'That's one of the reasons I don't have a rider,' I said. 'The idea of needing a go-between with the crew...it can cut you out. It's bad enough I don't get to go in the rig with everyone else.'

Rin nodded. 'I get that. But even from a distance, I always felt loyalty to my rig's dragon. I mean...the dragon practically *is* the rig. There would be no rig, and no crew, without a dragon to pull it. Rigs don't soar.'

'Well, I'm glad you think so,' I said. Privately, I thought there were humans who'd leap at the chance to replace us. And since society was already scaled for humans and not dragons, I didn't know where that would leave us. What we would do, if we couldn't pull rigs anymore.

Sometimes, I didn't know how it had come to this. History was full of stories of a time when humans had paid tribute to us, had begged us for safety and favours. When their royalty had considered us equals and petitioned for the chance to ride us in defence of their kingdoms. People had feared and loved us.

Now we were inconveniently opinionated packhorses.

I didn't like this line of thought. It drew too close to what Sar had said when she left. My crew was happy enough with me, and I was certainly happy with them so far. There was no point dwelling on it right now when there was work to do.

My crew paused to take in the splendour of the verdant cave. It had been foolish of us to see only the surface of one part of a planet and think it barren. I wondered if they were all re-evaluating, as I had been.

Then Vala walked the perimeter, bolt-gun in hand, checking for threats, while Boro headed for Scout Two, dragging a hovercart of our cargo with him. Rin and Finder, however, both crouched at the edge of a small pool of water, studying the little blob-creatures.

'Are they reacting?,' asked Rin. Their mech guided their gloved hand ever closer to a cluster of three of the blobs, which neither looked at Rin nor acknowledged their presence in any way.

Finder was not so shy, and scooped one up into its metal palms. 'They are unbothered. They appear somewhat gelatinous, and yet they have limbs and elements of structural shape,' said Finder. It gently stroked one on its blobby head; it jiggled when touched, but otherwise didn't move or react in any way. 'Are they certainly mobile?'

'Mech says there's one moving nearby,' said Rin. Finder immediately looked over to a little rock, where one of the creatures made its slow, jiggly way down toward a shallow pool of soaked moss.

'Fascinating,' said Finder.

'Do they look cute?,' asked Rin. They gently tickled the side of a blob with a gloved hand. 'They feel cute.'

'Extremely,' said Finder. 'They have variable colours as well. A rainbow of creatures.'

I thought about pushing for them to hurry up with the survey, then discarded it. What did it hurt if they enjoyed the wildlife here a bit? If anything, it might make them more willing to take care not to harm the ecosystem here.

I strode carefully across the cavern, occasionally splashing in the pools but not, I think, ever crushing any of the disc-lizards or blobs. I found a nice large rock to settle on, and once the disc-lizards had all skittered away from me, I laid down. I rested my head on my paws and curled my tail around me.

'All clear,' said Vala.

'Be on the lookout for cat-centipedes,' I said. 'They're cute but sneaky as fuck, and bigger than you are.'

'On it.'

What came next, I wasn't much part of. Boro and Rin helped Finder set up its survey equipment. Finder took samples from the cave and analysed the data from Scout Two. There was a lot of fiddling with tiny vials and miniscule bottles of chemicals, some of which absolutely reeked, but as interesting as it was to watch, I would only get in the way. My paws were too large and clumsy to handle things as small as that, and I was likely to inadvertently tip over their tables with my tail or when I stretched my wings if I wanted to get a closer look.

I contented myself with watching from a distance. The little blobs gradually made their way to me—I first noticed when one bumped my leg insistently. I sighed and carefully laid an open paw beside it. It climbed right on, heedless of my claws, each longer than the little creature.

It stared at me with its spot-like eyes, opening and closing its little mouth for a purpose I didn't understand—maybe just breathing—and I found it very hard to dislike it. 'I'm still not convinced you aren't some sort of weird little parasite,' I said. 'But you certainly *seem* friendly.'

When I put it down, it wandered off, and three more took its place, all wanting to be held, all, I assumed, studying me right back when I picked them up to look. It was a nice enough way to pass the time. The warier disc-lizards kept their distance, and I thought better of their judgement; while I would never knowingly hurt these creatures so long as they didn't threaten us, they had no way to know that. And additionally, they were so *small* that I was quite concerned about the humans accidentally stepping on them, let alone what I might accidentally do.

We confirmed that there was a deposit of vibroxis large enough for Finder's needs (still a modest amount, perhaps two pawfuls by my reckoning), and shallow, too, but there was a concern that extraction would upset the ecosystem here.

Personally, the more time I spent with these creatures, the more certain I was that we were not going to upset them, but it was neither my contract nor my call.

Eventually, Finder and Rin rigged something up that would extract the vibroxis but minimise vibrations and disturbance. As on a first test, neither the disc-lizards nor the blobs seemed to care, the extraction continued.

'It will likely take much longer,' Finder told me when the crew gathered to report. The extraction process was already set up, a large machine placed where Scout Two had previously probed. 'When we found it so quickly, I'd hoped we might have been able to be done with this within a day, but I expect this to take four days at least—five in local time, as their day-night cycle is faster.'

It didn't particularly worry me, as we were working on Finder's schedule, and the overtime was generous. 'Will that have a knock-on effect for our other extractions?'

Finder was silent for a moment. 'I do not believe so. Sufficient error time was included in my estimates.'

With that decided, it was a matter of finding somewhere sheltered for the rig—and me—to spend the night. Boro proved extremely helpful with this, sending the now superfluous Scout One in search of an appropriate and stable cave structure. I left Vala to guard the rest of the crew and checked out its result myself; a large, surface-level cave that was a bit of a squeeze for the rig on entry but opened out into plenty of room for me to curl up beside the rig without feeling cramped. There was even running water within the cave, though we'd need to test and purify it before drinking.

That night, we left the extraction running—though Finder was anxious about leaving it—and settled in our cave. A dust storm picked up over night but little of it reached us, and I sheltered behind the rig from the rest.

I stretched out onto my back with a sigh, examining the cracked ceiling of the cave here. Moss and roots clung to it, further evidence that most vegetation in this area was below-ground. I wondered whether there were blobs in a verdant cave nearby, perhaps accessible through paths that were merely hairline cracks to the rest of us.

I had taken my harness and helmet off. They were well-enough padded, but uncomfortable to wear overnight, and my back and wings were already scratched up enough thanks to that cat-thing. Finder had taken to calling it a 'felipede', but I thought cat-thing suited it better.

Now, the crew would all be unwinding after the long day, ready for sleep. Without my helmet, I didn't have easy access to their coms. I was alone now, properly alone for the first time since we'd set out.

I told myself that was a relief. I rolled onto my side, curled my tail tightly against my body, and went to sleep.

Chapter Eight

The next few days passed much the same way. Vala and I guarded the crew while Boro kept the rig in order and Finder and Rin worked on the vibroxis extraction, which as well as being a tediously slow process also required an enormous amount of supervision. Rin, it turned out, had quite the knack for analysis and computer maintenance, and they made an able assistant to Finder.

Vala needed more breaks than I had realised. She was so bold and competent that it was easy to forget that she had a chronic illness—until she grew waxen and sluggish and needed to rest wherever she was. With permission, I returned her to the rig on her worst days. She assured me that for her, this was normal. It didn't stop her from shooting a warning bolt to scare off the cat-thing twice in two days, her focus sharp when she was well.

The wildlife in the cave grew no more wary of us. On a lunch break, Rin came and sat beside me, eating their simple rig meal in its little compartmentalised tray. Though most of the crew still wore their hab-suits, helmets had become rarer when we were in the caves. Rin's hair was mussed and curly, their expression thoughtful. Their mech circled me, blinking its light as it scanned me.

At length, Rin asked, 'Are you holding a bunch of those blobs?' They gestured at the air with their spork.

'Does your mech not tell you?'

Rin shrugged. 'It does...but it's not always accurate, and I don't always have it on because it provides a lot of superfluous information. It's usually safer to ask.'

I looked down at the blobs all lined up on my paw and jiggling happily. 'Yeah. Well, they're sitting on me, anyway.'

'And how long has that been going on?'

I smiled at my collection of happy, fearless jellies. 'The whole time, pretty much. There's like twenty on my tail. Maybe. I've sort of lost count.'

Rin smiled down at their tray. 'They must be right at home with you.'

I snorted, smoke curling from my nostrils. 'I've been discouraging them from climbing higher because I don't want to lose them in my feathers.'

'You're like...furniture to them.'

'I *feel* like furniture,' I confided. 'But weirdly, not in a bad way.'

Rin nodded. 'I get that.'

'There's one of the lizards clinging to my back leg,' I added. 'Tickly little things.'

A blob bumped against Rin's boot. They felt it carefully, then picked it up and set it on their toe, where it jiggled peacefully. 'Maybe we're all furniture,' they said.

One day when we returned home and settled down for the night, Boro tapped the general rig com. 'Can you please stop leaving your used foodpacks around?! It's already attracting pests! If I have to chase one more of those disgusting crawler bugs out of here with one of your packs in its mandibles, I am going to lose it!'

'Sorry, Boro,' said Rin.

'Sorry, Boro,' said Vala.

Finder and I said nothing, as I ate separately and Finder's charging was zero-mess.

Boro sighed. 'Just...think about what you're doing. We all have to live here, and I'm the one cleaning up. And they got into my hormone pack yesterday.'

'Shit, I'm sorry,' said Vala, more sincerely this time. 'Do you have enough, still?'

'I do,' he said. 'They didn't take any *this time*.' His emphasis was clear.

Poor Boro. Hormone packs for gender transition were deeply personal.

After that, Vala tapped my com privately. 'He's like a fussy parent sometimes,' she said. 'I'm half-tempted to leave something out on purpose.'

'Don't,' I said, though I couldn't help but smile a little. 'He's not wrong.'

'Doesn't mean it wouldn't be funny,' she said, but as we didn't get another angry com from Boro the next day, I assumed she'd restrained herself.

Still, as I settled down for the night with my helmet removed and unable to hear the gentle chatter of my crew, loneliness closed in around me. It was a tight, trapped feeling, except that I was only trapped by and with myself.

When it had been me and Sar, she had come out to check on me every night. Or at least...for the first year or so, she had. She'd tell me all the little night-rituals the crew had done, amused by my eagerness to know. '*It's not so mysterious,*' she'd teased me. '*It's the same every night.*' She'd been unable to understand what it was like to be on the outside of my own crew. What it was like that my company every night had been only myself. Or how I had craved her predictable visits.

They say that dragons were solitary predators once. That we weren't really social with our own kind, or anyone else. Sometimes I felt that. That there was this invisible barrier between me and others, and every time I tried to breach it, it was seen as savagery. It was easier to be alone. But it wasn't what I wanted.

'Lux?'

Sar.

I rolled over, but it was only Rin. Their hab-suit was gone. They wore their longclothes, patterned with little stars, like a child might wear. 'Is something wrong?'

'No,' said Rin. They had a roll of something under their arm—a kit, maybe, in a tarp wrap. 'It's just our last night and...would you mind if I started a campfire?'

Campfire?

'Go ahead,' I said. 'There's a good bit of space between me and the rig. About where you are, actually.'

Rin knelt down and unrolled the kit. They set out some logs and little green blaze orbs, then started feeling around for rocks. Their mech shunted some toward their hands, and they formed a ring around the logs.

'I like to have a campfire sometimes,' they said. 'It reminds me of home.'

'Home?' I put my chin on my forepaws, curling my tail to encircle Rin and the nascent campfire without thinking.

Rin shrugged. 'I come from nomads,' they said. 'We live in landsailers, not hab-domes, so we can easily travel from place to place.'

'Starting fires?'

They smiled and started to stack their logs and sticks and orbs just so. 'For warmth, and light, and company,' they said. 'Fire is very important to us.'

'To dragons, too,' I said. I wondered what nomadic people Rin came from. The galaxy was a large place. But as they didn't volunteer it, I wasn't sure it was okay to ask.

My ears perked as they set a lighter to the blaze orbs, which immediately burst into flames, licking the bottoms of the logs with an audible, satisfying crackling sound. I'd never seen a human campfire like this; we dragons tend to make a big pile of stuff and flame it. I liked how methodical it was.

'Sounds like a big leap, from landsailers to void rigs.'

'Does it? My folk spend every night under the stars and travel with them as guides. You'll find as many of my folk on rigs as you'll find dragons, I think.'

I thought of Rin's poverty. Clothes worn to pieces, then carefully patched and embroidered in bright colours—boldly drawing attention to the repairs, rather than shamefully hiding them. I thought of their tribute, the coin necklace worn from their touch.

The campfire suddenly leapt into a broad flame, the green glow of the blaze orbs overwhelmed by the natural flame of the logs. Rin smiled and settled back, sitting across from me.

'What about you?' they asked. 'Are you from Ton?'

I nodded. 'I am. I guess my people are nomads too, but I was hatched on Ton and I can't seem to stop returning to it. Not so terribly far from Lema-dar, in fact.' I thought of the cave my mother had hatched me in—warm and earthy, padded with moss and lichen, nestled deep inside a mountain. Outside was not the brushland of Lema-dar but a dry forest rich with wildlife, and a small village that rarely saw rigs pass overhead but considered my mother a visiting hero, offering her tribute in the traditional way in exchange for her help dealing with predators and bandits.

She had many such villages on many planets—she called them her 'retirement plan'. But she remembered the names of those she helped, and asked after their children or parents when she visited, and I couldn't help but think she did care, at least a little. She'd encouraged me to do the same, but I didn't have it in me to make grand speeches, or look heroic. Or fight bandits or predators, for that matter. I was a merchant dragon to the bone.

I watched the fire burn down. We didn't talk much after that, but in a way that was entirely comfortable, with no expectations hanging in the air. When the logs were little more than embers, I looked up, expecting Rin to rally and return to the rig. Instead, they were curled up on their side, a foil-blanket wrapped around them. I wondered if they had any better blankets than the rig's standard issue foil ones. Perhaps I could knit them one, if I could ever get the yarn to work right.

I hesitated, then scooted closer to Rin, letting them borrow my heat. We dragons often get cold, but those close to us never do. I carefully shifted my tail so that it leaned against them, and the feather fan flopped over them.

They stirred, but didn't wake. I closed my eyes to the embers, to Rin's gentle, sleeping breaths, and fell asleep less lonely than I had in months.

⟨ ⟩

I woke to Finder watching the pair of us. As ever, its expressionless face was unreadable.

'Is everything alright?' I asked, stretching and getting to my paws. Below me, Rin sighed and rolled over.

'The extraction is complete,' it said. 'We just need to collect the equipment and material for transport now.'

'Oh. That's great news.' I padded around Rin, hoping the click of my claws against the cave floor wouldn't wake them. I picked up my harness and started to clip it on, but Finder still stared at me.

With Finder, I found it best to be direct. 'Why are you staring at me?'

'I am thinking,' it replied, typically vague.

'Are you thinking about me?'

'Yes.'

'What are you thinking about me?' I asked, digging my claws into the stone. A nervous habit that terrified humans.

Finder didn't look terrified. 'I am thinking that my colleague, Onna, was right about dragons. And that I was wrong about you.'

I didn't know how to take that, and I was fast tiring of trying to understand. 'Whatever. Let's go get this vibroxis and say goodbye to Hazanthis.'

'Yes,' said Finder. 'That is the natural course of action.'

It didn't take us long to get up and ready to load up the vibroxis. Rin appeared among the crewmates, suited up and ready, as if they'd spent the night in the rig as normal. Finder made no further comment, but I did often turn to find it staring at me with the same intensity it had while analysing scout data.

Finder and Rin packed up the equipment and carefully strapped the canisters of vibroxis to our hovercart. Boro constantly tapped our coms, fretting over the state of the rig and how little time he had to get it perfect, while Vala said farewell to the blobs that had become our companions over the last few days.

'Stay strong,' she said to the three blobs in her hands. They opened and closed their mouths silently in response, mimicking talking. 'Don't let anything eat you. Unless you're into that, I guess. I still have no idea how you can survive like this.'

'Maybe everything else is as charmed by them as we are,' I said, letting several blobs march off my forepaw and onto a rock. 'Maybe sometimes the universe is gentle.'

Vala gave me a strange look, but said, 'Yeah. Maybe.' Then she smiled and said, 'Thanks for taking me on, boss. It's been a good job so far.'

I went out first to clear the way for my crew, treading air while they pushed the hovercart up the cliffside. My eyes caught movement; a many-legged cat clung to the side of the rockface, fresh scars on its sides and shoulders. Its gaze followed my crew with predatory intensity.

I flew forward, grabbing the side of the cliff beside it, thrust my face into its, and growled, smoke pouring from my nostrils and between my teeth. The cat-thing stared at me, then skittered up and away. I watched it flee into the distance. Good.

'It's still kinda cute,' I muttered.

Chapter Nine

We left Hazanthis and made for Oglod, where Finder had sourced another incredibly rare material: glodium. As the planet did have people living on it in one tiny village, we stopped there first to ask for trade or, failing that, permission to extract.

Static crackled through my feathers on approach to the village, Haven. The atmosphere had been shrouded in thick, icy clouds, through which we saw a planet that was predominately snow-speckled plains. However, Haven was in the midst of a thick forest not far from a small stretch of lake coast, shielding them from the worst of the weather.

'It looks quaint,' I said through coms, taking in the small, blocky habs with garden rooftops and the bright cobbled streets.

'Quaint's bad,' Vala replied.

'No it isn't,' said Rin.

'It is. These people didn't settle on a shithole planet at the edge of the galaxy for no reason. Trust me.'

I didn't think they'd come here for no reason, but I didn't see why it had to be a *bad* reason. Boro hailed their com tower (well, com shack) and requested permission to land.

'Land lakeside, and none too close,' came the crackly reply.

There was a worn stretch of dirt marked with faded white paint that I took to be their docking site. I detached from the rig and Rin piloted it in for landing; they were fast becoming our go-to pilot for things like this, using readings from the scanners to land rather than sight, and doing so more carefully than a fully-sighted pilot might.

I fanned my wings as I landed, careful not to gouge the ground with my claws or skid too much. The energy of the Haven's com operator didn't feel particularly welcoming, and I didn't want to give them any reason to resent us.

My crew joined me outside, Vala emerging with her bolt-gun in hand and her glass blades sheathed at her hips. I put one ear forward and one-back at the sight. 'Are all those weapons necessary?' I asked her. It was one thing to go armed when we were in the wilderness, but we were in a marked clearing outside a thriving village.

Vala gave me a level look. 'We don't know these people.'

'You should put them back,' said Boro. 'We'll put them on edge.'

'Good!'

'Bad,' said Rin. 'We need their blessing to extract.'

It was hard to imagine anyone in the village could pose a threat to *me*. 'Vala, I trust your judgement when it comes to security, but I agree with Rin and Boro. We don't want to come off as dangerous. Leave the weapons behind.'

'I'll put my bolt-gun away,' said Vala.

'And your swords,' said Boro.

'And one sword.'

'No swords,' I said firmly.

Vala made a half-growl, half-hiss, like an angry cat. 'Fine, boss! But I'm keeping my knives.'

As she stomped back to the rig, Rin asked, 'She has knives?'

'Believe me, it's news to me, too,' I said. I couldn't help but feel fondly toward Vala even in her grumpiness. She worked hard to keep us safe, even though she was already transitioning from a security role to a crew one due to her illness. Boro worried she ruffled too many feathers to be part of a social expedition, but my feathers were unruffled, and I wanted her with us.

A cluster of some five humans appeared at the edge of the village and made their way toward us. I noted they had bolt-guns.

Well. They didn't have a dragon to guard them, as my crew did. I wouldn't hold it against them.

'Any opinions?' I asked Finder.

Though Finder did not emote as humans did, I read surprise in its pause. 'You are experienced in this kind of work and I am not. My opinion is irrelevant outside the extraction process.'

'I'd like to know anyway, if you don't mind,' I said.

'Fear of the unknown is powerful. I believe empathy will serve us better than assertiveness.'

'How do we gain their empathy?'

Finder's gaze was fixed on the approaching trio. 'It is about giving, not gaining,' it said.

I flicked the fan of my tail, contemplating.

The trio stopped a dragon's length from us. It seemed to me that they aimed to be out of range of my flame. Had they encountered hostile dragons? They were dressed in layers of light fabric and knitwear, though spun from unfamiliar materials.

'I'm Undara,' said the first of the trio, a burly woman with piercings armouring her ears, nose, and cheeks. Her companions were also pierced, but not as extensively. Their gazes lingered on Finder the longest. 'What's your business here?'

There was a pause, and I realised with a start that my crew was waiting for *me* to speak. 'We're traders,' I said, though I wondered if that was strictly true. Our crew and contract was rather different from the other merchant rigs I had known. 'I'm Luxorian and this is my crew. We've come asking for permission to trade or extract glodium.'

I looked to my crew for approval. Sar would have said something more warm, and would have smiled and played with her hair. I didn't have hair and I didn't think these tense folk would react well to me baring my teeth.

Rin listened intently, their mech resting on their shoulder and no doubt giving them a description of the villagers. Vala's mouth was set in a sullen line and her arms were crossed. But Boro caught my eye, then nodded minutely toward Undara. I couldn't make out what he wanted. Was I supposed to say something more? Walk closer?

Boro took a step toward Undara and said, 'We have need of some supplies, too, and plenty we'd be willing to trade for it.'

'Haven has no need of credits,' said Undara.

'But barter and services, perhaps, might be useful,' he said. 'Besides, we'd love to share news and stories with your folk. I'm sure we have much to learn and we'd be grateful for new company. Company isn't too varied on a void rig.'

Undara's companions looked to each other and murmured something I couldn't make out even when I pricked my ears. A benefit of them standing at shouting distance, no doubt.

'We don't know you,' said Undara. 'We cannot grant extraction rights to strangers. But we'll see if your barter or stories are worth anything. You may enter the village. You'll have to sleep in your rig.'

'Thank you,' I said. 'We're grateful for your hospitality.'

Undara nodded and left, her companions flanking her.

I perked an ear at Boro. 'Our company isn't good enough?'

'It was just friendly banter,' said Boro. 'You might try it.' He smiled, taking the sting from his words.

Frankly, I was glad I had Boro so I didn't have to.

I'd thought the locals would be excited for visitors, as isolated as they were, but people kept their distance, whispering behind their hands. Boro spoke with people here and there but I held back; if they were nervous, they didn't need a dragon looming over them. I hadn't forgotten the way Undara and her companions had stopped beyond range of firebreath.

It was Finder that seemed to really draw them out. All eyes fixed on it. If Finder noticed, it gave no sign.

When there was a flash and click as someone took an image of it, I turned my head to the bot. 'Are they bothering you?' I kept my voice low, my head near the bot. It's not easy for a dragon to be quiet, but I did my best.

Finder considered the humans still gawking at it. 'I don't believe they've seen bots before. I see no sign of bots or even mechs here.'

That *was* odd. Bots might not have chosen to live so far from civilisation; the population here was tiny, after all. But mechs were non-sentient machines that were useful in nearly all contexts; one only needed to look to Rin to see one of their many uses.

'Do you think they have some kind of automaton prejudice?'

'Given their fascination with me, I doubt it. Perhaps they do not have anyone here with the requisite skills to maintain mechs. I'll inform Boro; perhaps that will be a useful angle to pitch our services.'

I nodded. 'And...are they bothering you, though?' The bot hadn't answered. Typically evasive of it.

'Not presently.'

'Let me know if they do,' I said. 'You shouldn't have to put up with all this scrutiny.'

Finder was quiet for a moment. 'I will.'

《 》

They were not quick to warm to strangers, however many images they took of us and however much they stared. Over the next week, Boro proved invaluable. He won over the villagers with jokes and good cheer, instructing us to do similarly.

As we sat outside at their quaint pub—none of their buildings were large enough to accommodate me, but the garden was—I considered the villagers. Many were outside with us, though whether to keep us company or to enjoy the clear weather, I couldn't say.

Vala nudged Boro. 'They really like you.'

'Of course,' said Boro. 'They're friendly enough folk.'

'They are not,' said Rin. 'When I said hello to someone yesterday, they spat at my feet.'

'Well...they're friendly enough once you get to know them,' he said. 'And they like Finder, too.'

'I believe they do not like me as a person so much as find me a fascinating novelty,' said Finder. 'Hardly anyone has had a proper conversation with me.'

Boro rubbed the back of his neck. 'It's...look, sometimes you just have to grit your teeth and keep trying with people. People want to be friendly, you know? I think that's basically true.'

'That has not been my experience,' said Rin.

'I don't want to be friendly,' said Vala.

'I tried to be friendly to Rin at the Tribute Fair,' I offered.

Rin rolled their eyes. 'And gave everyone a good laugh at my expense.'

'Fine!' Boro threw up his hands. 'Present company excluded.'

'You know, Boro,' I put my head on my paws, 'I'd begun to expect that you weren't actually charming. But you've really proven yourself with these Oglodians.'

Boro looked like he was ageing just from talking to me. 'Was that...a compliment or an insult?'

'A compliment!' I insisted. 'Why would you think...oh, because I said I thought you weren't charming? But that's just what I was thinking before.'

'This is what I get for signing on with an autistic dragon, I suppose,' said Boro.

'And a bot,' said Finder.

'And an autistic crewmate,' said Rin.

Vala raised her hand. 'I'm neurotypical, actually. I just don't like people.'

'But we appreciate you,' I said. 'You're a great crew member, and we need someone who's good with people. We'd be lost without you.'

'And our rig would be a tip,' said Vala.

'Bah,' said Boro, but he ducked his head and tried to hide a pleased smile.

《 》

The Oglodians, as it turned out, did not have any glodium they were willing to trade. But they were willing to grant us a permit to extract a specific amount, for a specific period, provided our methods met with the approval of their environmental officer. Like most lightly inhabited planets that weren't being cored by corporate entities, the Oglodians were doing their best to ensure Oglod would survive and thrive well into the future.

The rest of our time on Oglod, however, was less than pleasant; its wildlife wasn't nearly as mild as Hazanthis, and its sudden hail storms were powerful enough to pock the metal of the rig, and likely shred the humans' hab-suits—or my feathers and exposed dragon flesh—in time. My human crew complained of the air pressure messing with their hair, Finder was reluctant to emerge at all, and I had to admit that the climate was wreaking havoc on my feathers. We couldn't quite find a cave, but sheltered beneath a cliff. I helped the crew erect some barriers of tarp and metal, under Finder's direction.

Vala had to shoot at something trying to eat the humans at least once a day—thankfully, she was as good a shot as she'd claimed. I worried a lot more when she tired than I had on Hazanthis. And I had a clash with a giant four-winged bat-thing that was even larger than I was, and an awful lot meaner. I took to sheltering with the crew rather than taking wing, to avoid attracting more of its kind.

Rin did not sleep out with me again. I didn't know whether that was by preference or simply because it was too dangerous. I didn't feel particularly safe myself. I took frequent light naps rather than my preferred deep sleep, keeping a wary eye out for bad-tempered bat-monsters.

I had been sad to see the back of Hazanthis' little blobs and lizards, but I'd have gladly flipped my tail at the whole of Oglod if I could have. I felt nothing but relief when we took to the winds again and left.

Chapter Ten

Our last stop was Byroda, a lumpy blue-green orb with a sickly green atmospheric glow. Electrical storms crackled across the planet.

'How bad are the storms?' I asked across coms.

'I don't know what to make of these readings,' said Rin.

'They *look* fucking nightmarish,' said Vala.

I fanned my wings to slow, feathers catching on strands of shining wind; Boro threw on the reverse thrusters to match me.

There was a crackle as Finder joined the com. 'The entire atmosphere is electrified, but only the large storms will cause us issue. We can safely descend elsewhere.'

'What kind of issue?' I asked.

'The rig is likely to lose power due to energy overload. You might also experience mild to moderate electrocution.'

There was a pause as we all considered this.

'Is electrocution something that can be mild?' asked Boro.

'Of course,' said Finder. 'Severe electrocution causes death.'

'We avoid the storms,' I said. 'I don't want to find out what mild electrocution feels like.'

The crew chorused their agreement and we breached the atmosphere far from the storms. Byroda, it turned out, was an extremely wet planet dominated by swamps, bogs, and swampy, boggy oceans. Well, there were rainforests and lush mountains as well, but it was a swamp we needed if we were going to find any mitanite, according to Finder.

'Everything here reeks!' I said, closing my nostrils as if I was underwater. The whole planet was pervaded with a foul stench.

'I don't smell anything,' said Boro.

'We're in an airtight void rig,' said Rin.

'Right.'

'What's the smell?' asked Vala.

I considered. 'I can only describe it as "if a garbage heap farted".'

Vala snorted. 'Delicious.'

'Yeah, well, make sure you close your nostrils.' Even with my nostrils closed, it felt like the smell was still getting through. Maybe my nose was already full of stink and it was too late for me. I closed my third eyelid as well in case my eyes were to blame somehow.

'Humans can't close our nostrils,' said Rin.

'Oh. Well, wear a helmet or this is gonna suck for you.'

It turned out what we needed was in the foulest swamp we could find. 'Mitanite is known as "the stinky mineral",' Finder told us, plenty cheerful from its position of being able to turn off its smell sensors. 'Mitanite once belonged to Byroda's gaseous moon before it exploded thousands of years ago.'

I found myself grateful we weren't extracting from a stinky moon instead, but was nonetheless grumpy about our miserable circumstances.

'Who knows?' I murmured to myself. 'Maybe Byroda will grow on me.'

〈 〉

Byroda was a trash heap of a planet. It did not grow on me. However, I did end up with quite a lot of it on my feathers.

I spent our entire stay weighed down by mud and misery, my feathers and legs absolutely thick with the stuff. I didn't get used to the smell; if anything, it got worse every day.

It took longer than planned, too. Finder struggled with the swamp, which clogged up its gears and threatened its equipment. Technically, bots and computers were both waterproof, but mudproof was a whole other problem.

Boro was also in a terrible mood. Keeping the rig shining and ready was something he considered his personal responsibility, and now preventing it from sinking was the first step, never mind keeping mud and swamp water out of the landing gear. He looked absolutely exhausted any time I looked at him, and he had very little to say to anyone, but he didn't complain...out loud. Everyone stepped lightly around him, and Vala confided to me on private com that she'd been taking extra care around the rig, wiping everything down and putting things away, because she thought if Boro found an unwashed mug on a counter he might actually pass out from the stress.

But the wildlife on Byroda was pretty small and unthreatening. We weren't in deep enough mud or water to fear the crab-sharks that hunted their oceans—which I was very glad of, because they were easily three times the size of me—and most of the creatures we did encounter were frightened of the humans, let alone me. Insect-like creatures about the size of squirrels watched us from the trees, clinging with their chitinous claws and staring from multiple jewel-like eyes. They did not seem particularly brave, and never ventured near enough to smell, let alone touch.

But for all it was miserable, the weather was mild. The first night, Rin brought out their campkit and blanket again. 'Mind if I join you?'

I lifted my head hopefully. 'No, not at all.'

They picked their way across the ground; all of us had been learning where the ground was more solid to avoid constantly wading through mud. Rin, more used to uncertain ground, was learning faster than the rest of us. Though for me, there was almost no help for it anyway.

I was on a large patch of hard ground now, where the stone was close to the surface and it was a bit raised compared to the rest of the swamp. Patches big enough for me were few and far between, and genuine pathways were out of the question. But if I took to the air, I'd shower the entire area in mud.

As Rin set up the campfire, they asked, 'How're you holding up?'

'Well. I'm up,' I said. 'All my feathers are stuck together, my legs are fully brown now, and I'm starting to worry I'll never be clean again. But this is just temporary.' I paused. 'Unless I really can't get it off but I'm trying not to think about that.'

'It comes off,' said Rin. They lit the fire, which started green from the spheres then sparked into a rush of orange flame. 'It...takes a lot of scrubbing. We all spend a lot more time in the shower here.'

'That's something I miss from my hab-dome,' I said. I started to curl my tail around Rin, then realised I'd shower them in mud and resisted. 'Rigs don't come with dragon-friendly showers. We're expected to bathe in the wild when we're travelling.'

'We could hose you down,' Rin suggested. 'We definitely have a hose.'

'Hmm.' The difficulty was, the rig's water system was self-cleaning and recycling. If they sprayed it all over me, then we'd fast run out of water as it'd all just be swallowed by the swamp.

'We can filter this stuff,' said Rin. 'Really, it's doable.' They hesitated. 'Well...maybe not *this* stuff. But there's murky water as well as mud; we can filter *that*.'

'That'd be nice,' I said. 'It's been one day and I already barely remember what it feels like to be clean.'

'Room for a few more?' Vala called from the rig. The other members of our crew picked their way out to the campfire.

'Of course,' I said. I shifted a little, trying to leave them a bit more room to sit without sinking into the mud that surrounded my little island of hard ground.

The humans spread a large tarp and sat down, each with their own blankets and bundles—I noticed Boro's was a flowery crochet, and Vala's a thick, practical quilt, compared to Rin's foil blanket. Finder remained standing, which didn't surprise me. It was disgusted by the swamp and had mentioned before that standing was significantly less uncomfortable for most bots than it was for organic creatures.

Boro wrapped his blanket more tightly around his shoulders. 'I hope you won't take Rin sleeping out here into consideration when choosing your rider, Luxorian. I would have been out on Hazanthis, too, had I known.' He aimed a glare at Rin.

I was about to squash *that* idea, when Rin said, 'Lux doesn't need a rider, Boro. Just a crew.'

Need, not want. Something about that warmed me.

It had been going well, hadn't it? This big experiment, as daunting as it had first seemed, was close to being a complete success. All we had to do was get the mitanite off this stinky planet and back to Finder's colleague on Bas-Ros Station, and it would be over. I'd have my rig, and proof that I could do this alone.

Well. I looked around at my crew, chatting and bickering around the fire with the comfort of familiarity. Not alone. I hoped they'd stay on with me. I knew Boro was looking to become a rider though, and there would be more Tribute Fairs before the year was up. And of course Finder would go back to work on Bas-Ros...

If Rin and Vala stayed, maybe that would be enough.

They stayed with me long into the night, until the logs were embers, then ashes. I dozed to the sounds of their voices, and when I woke, only Rin was left, sleeping comfortably under the stars. Every night after that, they all came and had a campfire with me until it was time to sleep. The rig no longer separated me from my crew.

I thought about what Rin had said on Hazanthis, about me *being* the rig. Though rigs couldn't soar without a dragon, I had always felt more like a minor component, easily ignored. But now, with my crew choosing to spend their nights with me even out in the mud and stink, I felt important in a way I never had before.

When we finally extracted the mitanite, the whole crew cheered, and I cheered with them, sending a spurt of flame into the sky. We were finally done with Byroda, nearly done with the whole contract, and there were still a few days left in our original two week estimate.

Though Finder was footing the bill for the contract and any overtime, it suggested we find a river to wash me clean. It was a little awkward at first, being scrubbed and hosed down by the crew, but it was also nice. Boro fussed over making sure my feathers were kept in good order. Rin was careful not to get water in my eyes or anywhere sensitive, checking in constantly. Vala was suffering from exhaustion and had to rest in the rig, but instructed the others over coms with surprising knowledge of where the mud was likely to accumulate.

When we finally took off, seeking the faint threads of the shining winds, I was clean and fresh and felt cared for in a way I hadn't in years, since long before Sar had left me.

I fanned out my wings, catching the light, feeling the shining winds as they rushed through my feathers. Electricity built up inside me and spread out through my feathers, crackling and heady.

And then I was soaring, and the void was consumed in the rush of the winds, pink and flowing. I curled my forepaws against my chest, enjoying the familiar beauty of the winds and the comfort of knowing we'd soon be at Bas-Ros Station and back to civilization.

Rin tapped my com. 'All well?'

'All good,' I replied. I hesitated. 'Would...would it be alright if the rig opened general coms to me?'

I heard Boro chuckle.

'Already open, boss,' said Vala.

I settled in for a pleasant flight in good company. Then a shadow passed along the winds to my left.

Chapter Eleven

'We're dropping,' I said. 'Get ready. There's something here.' My chest was tight, my breathing laboured. I needed to move fast. The shadow was growing darker and larger by the moment.

I bated my wings, beating backwards. The winds faded away and the void snapped into place. Unfamiliar space, unfamiliar planets.

'Where are we?' I said tightly. 'Boro?'

'Map's calibrating...'

I looked around, treading empty space, my feathers swirling around me. The tethers to the rig hung loose; I stroked forward once, just to feel them go taut and reassure myself they were still secured to my harness.

Dropping out of the shining winds avoided cosmic horrors hunting there nearly every time. Though they could perceive dragons and rigs as we soared, they weren't good at tracking us when we stopped.

Most of the time.

I paused, taking in the space around us. A bright red gas planet lit with atmospheric electricity and three shadow moons. A distant green planet that looked utterly smooth and glass-like.

'Map is up!' said Boro. 'We're in the Vyar system.'

The Vyar system. I tried to pin-point my location in my mind. Dragons did not have maps that we could easily consult while flying. I could take out my com and look at it, but that was risky in space and anyway, the screen would still be frustratingly small. Like most dragons, my education had had a strong focus on chorography and memorisation.

Vyar. That meant the gas planet was Volcos, and the glassy green one was Mith. I centred myself on a vast map in my mind, made up not so much of planets but of the winds that bound them. A fixed point within the constant flow.

There.

I knew where we were.

I knew how to fly to Bas-Ros Station.

'Boss, we're detecting something big.' Rin's voice was strained.

I swirled on the spot, taking in our surroundings.

A shadow passed over us as I turned.

Long, many-jointed limbs ended in floppy, curling fingers. Black flesh pitted with countless bloodshot eyes, fluttering and shifting like flies on a carcass. Instead of a body, a vast, misshapen head, like a human's but with mouths instead of eyes. It bared its teeth from all three mouths, revealing rows upon rows of broken yellow teeth, each tooth as thick as my neck. It squatted in space like a hideous spider, like a squid stuffed with bones.

It reached for me with seventeen oddly fluid hands.

I hit the buttons on my chestplate in sequence, manually triggering the tether release. 'Head for Volcos,' I said. Horrors couldn't tolerate most atmospheres. They were twisted things that haunted the void and the winds only.

'Boss—'

'Lux—'

'You can't—'

'GO!' I roared, and flame gathered in my fire pouch. I fanned my wings, catching the sunlight, catching the subtle threads of the winds, and flew to meet the horror.

With luck, my crew hadn't looked at it for long. Humans couldn't always tolerate horrors. I'd known more than one crew member who had broken on seeing a horror and had never returned to the void again.

I wasn't fond of it myself. It made my feathers prickle. But I was a dragon and the shining winds were *mine*. This horror had no right to chase me from them.

I ducked under three floppy hands and wove between its flaccid arms, threads of the winds lending me speed even here. The horror was ponderously slow, but its flickering fly-like eyes followed my every move with rapt attention, and it had more arms than I could easily track. As another vast, wriggling appendage swung at me, I used the winds to kick up above it only for a vast hand to close on me from above.

A thing I had been warned of from a hatchling was to never let a horror get a grip on you. They were horribly strong and a dragon couldn't find the winds from within their grasp. I would be pulped and then sucked up like a meat smoothie.

I twisted in its still-closing grasp, claws raking the rubbery flesh that split and oozed black pus. It didn't so much as flinch, those boneless fingers tightening around me.

I tried to flame but my fire couldn't catch in the void. I brought up my hind legs and wrapped myself around one of the fingers, ripping and tearing in every direction with teeth and claws both. The horror's ichor burned like acid as it splattered my muzzle and coated my mouth.

I wrenched my head again and felt something tear; the finger ripped free and I rushed out into the space it left. The horror keened, a cry that was simultaneously a high and human-like scream and something deep and gravelly.

More hands reached for me, wriggling toward me from all directions; I tucked my wings and spiralled away from them and around the back of the horror's head. Its many eyes were still fixed on me; just as many on the back as the front. Its arms tangled around each other as they followed, moving not as appendages so much as individual eels. They were slower than I was and many had reached their limit. I swooped below the horror and then back up, flaring my wings to look at the enormous, three-mouthed face that made up its entire torso. The mouths gnashed rows and rows of long, jagged teeth of variable length. They seemed to shred themself as they did so, the flesh around the mouths cloudy with pus.

I shuddered, feathers shivering, then flew straight at it, aiming not for the mouths but the eyes surrounding them. I kicked and scratched everything I could, raking my claws across them. The bulbous orbs burst beneath my claws and the horror keened again, this time wild and staccato with panic. More hands grabbed for me but I was much too fast, eviscerating more eyes as I went. The void went murky in my wake, full of oily ichor.

The horror grew more frantic, no longer reaching for me but flailing. One arm caught me and sent me spinning out into space. I tried to straighten my wings and find purchase again on the winds. As I did, I watched the horror retreat, becoming a shadow in space and then disappearing into the void.

I panted, taking stock of myself. My face and paws burned, as well as several patches on my wings, but nothing I couldn't bear.

I tapped the rig's com. 'It's gone,' I said, half-wondering whether they would hear me. Whether some of the horror's vile ooze had eaten into my coms array.

A pause and then the broken response from Boro: 'We're safe, boss. We're orbiting the other side of Volcos.'

I looked at the red planet. Part of me hated that they hadn't broken the atmosphere, where they'd be safe. As I'd asked them to, no less. Another part was glad they'd be easy to find. 'On my way,' I said, angling my wings to catch the right thread of the winds.

'Are you okay?' asked Rin.

'How did you get rid of it?' asked Vala.

'I'm fine. And I scratched the shit out of it,' I said.

When I rejoined my crew and they got a look at me through the rig's windows, there was a lot of fussing and concern, which was misplaced but gratifying. As uncomfortable as I was with the horror's ichor burning me, it was bearable, and I made it clear I'd much rather get safely to Bas-Ros to clean off than land on one of these low population planets and potentially have to fight off even more monsters.

I hooked myself back up to the rig's tethers, took a moment to get my bearings in the vastness of the void, and soared, the void consumed by the pink light of the winds.

The rest of the journey was quiet; though I remained alert for horrors, nothing loomed over us. More than once, I saw fleeting shadows in my peripheral vision, but they were quickly left behind.

I warned my crew and we stopped soaring in the Lutanier system, with the overlapping, spinning rings of Bas-Ros Station shining in the distance, lit blue at one side from the shine of the crystal planet it orbited. Other dragons pulled rigs in and out, some soaring the moment they pulled away, others sailing comfortably toward the planet's surface.

I manoeuvred my rig through the rings, searching for one of the many blue port windows, and sure enough one spun slowly up toward me; a wide entrance covered in a stable blue forcefield. I made for it, taking note of which way up everything inside seemed to be. There was nothing worse than entering a station upside-down and the gravity yanking you onto your back.

I flew in smoothly, the rig gliding in behind. I landed, taking only a few hopping steps to come to a halt, and disengaged the rig tethers. I'd been through this entrance before, or one just like it; docking bays lined the walls for rigs of all kinds, and a few other dragons made their way deeper into the station. There were humans and bots everywhere, but not milling around in chat; instead they all criss-crossed the port, making lines toward the rigs, the officials and repair workers lining the edges, or following their dragons out.

Rather than making my own way out, I waited for my crew, claws tapping repeatedly on the floor as the stream of humans and bots parted around me. At length, Rin tapped my com. 'We've docked. Boro wants to settle the port fee; apparently he's well-known at Bas-Ros and expects a discount. I told him to clear it with you first.'

I was pleased Rin had thought to check, though of course I wouldn't say no to a discount. 'He's clear,' I said. 'I'll pay him back when he's done.'

If Rin thought Boro was likely to inflate the fee for his own benefit, they didn't mention it. I wasn't terribly worried, myself. I expected a port like this to cost about ten credits for a few days docked. As long as I paid Boro that or less, what did it matter if Boro made a bit of coin in the exchange?

When Boro arrived, he'd got us a full week for five credits less than I'd expected to pay for two or three days, which was frankly astounding. I'd long-since lost my image of Boro as a charmer or smooth-talker, but he was certainly good at making friends.

'Is there a decontam unit here?' I asked. Though I'd been willing to bear the horror's bile for the sake of making port sooner, the vile pus was starting to burn and the stench of it lit my nose on fire.

'Already looked it up. Vala's going to take you to it and Boro and I will meet you there.'

'Vala?'

'Hey, boss.' Vala gave me a tight smile. It had been a while since I'd seen her without her armoured hab-suit; she was wearing another boiler suit, this one purple with the top tied around her waist. She'd left her bolt-gun behind, but her void-glass swords hung from a strap over her shoulder. 'You stink worse than moof piss.'

'Think how much worse it is for me,' I said. 'This shit is on my *face*.'

'This way to a clean shower,' said Vala.

'I'll arrange for the materials to be sent to my colleague,' said Finder. After a moment, it said, 'Done. How may I assist?'

The decontam unit was little more than a large tiled room with special drainage and a big hose, but my crew made it work. They all put on special hazard suits, even Finder, so that the horror bile wouldn't eat away at them, and they hosed me down properly. It was a lot more painful than it had been when they helped me wash on Byroda; my skin had developed burns, and some of my feathers had melted together. To my surprise, it was Vala who salved the burns and carefully extracted the damaged feathers, putting med gel on the puckered papillae to staunch the bleeding.

'You've patched up a dragon before,' I said. I'd thought her experienced when I first met her, too, though she'd claimed otherwise.

Vala shrugged. 'I worked with the Cosmic Defenders. Let's leave it at that.'

With the horror bile safely sloughed off and my wounds dressed, my body was relieved. But anxiety sloshed around my gut, like I'd swallowed rotten meat.

Chapter Twelve

We made our way out of the docks and into the station proper. Inside, it felt like nothing so much as an enclosed city, though it was a city without a sky where both the ceiling and the floor were streets lined with tall buildings. It was crowded; dragons, humans, and bots alike travelled on foot or by craft alongside various livestock and beasts of burden. I could see a fluffy, pig-like mufflia and two swaying, stick-legged veemas just within our immediate periphery. Everything was brightly lit. We'd arrived in the midst of an artificial day-cycle, and the greys and browns of the buildings were washed in a warm, sunny yellow.

Something I really didn't like about Bas-Ros Station was that a dragon couldn't spread their wings. There was room enough, but the artificial gravity flipped mid-way, making it dangerous, and if *all* the dragons here flew, we would fast run out of air. It was rare that I felt trapped; afterall, even my hab-dome in Lema-dar was just a few short steps from open sky. Not even a planet could hold a dragon. But Bas-Ros Station was both large and tightly contained. I wondered whether my crew shared my discomfort, but if they did they hid it well. Finder, Vala, and Boro chatted companionably as we walked, and Rin listened in with no more than their usual amount of awkward tension.

But then, Bas-Ros had been *built* for them. For all dragons pulled the rigs that had transported everyone here, for all dragons had been integral to even being able to construct this place at all, Bas-Ros didn't *feel* like much thought had been given to the dragons that would live or travel here. Most of the buildings had been built to a humanoid scale. The streets, while wide enough for dozens of humans to pass comfortably, couldn't admit more than three dragons abreast without us choking up traffic. And of course, we couldn't fly here, though no dragon would build a station without room to fly.

Why had our society been created like this? Ever since Sar had abandoned me, I'd noticed it more and more. Humans and dragons were inseparable; our histories had been intertwined since before it was even recorded. But humans were *reliant* on us: to protect them, to transport them. And with their clever little hands, they'd built a world that made *us* reliant on them.

I was glad, at least, that *my* crew accepted me as an individual in my own right. As their boss, no less. But the rest of the galaxy—even other dragons!—would forever ask me *'Where's your rider?'*

Finder stopped outside a large, run-down, warehouse-like building and turned to face us. I noticed the doors were large enough to comfortably admit a dragon, though that was likely just a bonus to making it large enough to admit various transporters and vehicles.

'This is where my colleague, Onna, and I have been working,' said Finder. It hesitated, something I wasn't used to seeing it do. 'Our work requires the utmost secrecy,' it said. 'If you wish to see it, then I must ask you to sign a non-disclosure agreement.'

Boro snorted. 'Really, Finder?'

'I insist,' said Finder. 'You will be paid whether you enter or not. But if you wish to know what we've been collecting materials for, you must swear, in writing, that you will not reveal what you've seen to anyone until such time as I or Onna dissolves the agreement.'

Working for Finder thus far hadn't bothered me. Finder had maintained its secrecy, but it had also been an exemplary member of the crew, helping not just with the extractions but also with repairs and maintenance and just generally being a companion to us all. I *liked* Finder.

I was now reminded of how dodgy the contract had been and just how large a carrot it had dangled in order to get me to sign up in spite of my misgivings.

It wasn't that I could imagine Finder doing something truly heinous—building weapons, or...or torturing people. My mind drew a blank, trying to picture Finder causing harm to *anyone*.

But though I liked and trusted Finder, I hadn't known it for very *long*. And that whole time, it had been keeping secrets from me. To add this lack of trust on top of everything put a sting in my gizzard.

I dug my claws into the ground, scraping them against the hard concrete.

'I'll sign,' said Rin.

I glanced at them in surprise, my ears flicking back. Rin tapped their com to Finder's and listened in silence for a few minutes before saying, clearly, 'Rin Loe.'

'Yeah, me too,' said Vala. She barely glanced at the contract before inputting her own name.

Boro and I glanced at each other. If he'd had a tail, I was sure it would be swishing just like mine. Boro and I had the experience to know when something was off.

I just wished I had a little bit more, so that I could tell *why*.

I thought about how Finder had sought me out—me, specifically, not looking to deal with my rider. Not assuming I had a rider at all.

I read through the contract. It seemed to be standard enough...

I awkwardly input my name into the contract using the scroll-wheel on my com. 'I'd like to see,' I said firmly.

Boro groaned and pinched his nose. 'Really?'

I shrugged a wing. 'You don't have to sign.'

'And be the only one who doesn't?' said Boro. 'Like some kind of...outcast?'

Rin snorted.

Boro glanced at the contract, surely too fast to take it in, and input his name as well. 'There. Nobody's leaving me out!'

Finder stared at Boro a moment. Its face was bot-still and yet, I could not help but feel, was surely concealing the same general confusion around Boro that I felt all the time.

I'd expected to walk in and find Onna at work with all our new materials, but it turned out this warehouse was actually made up of several smaller warehouses. Finder led us such a labyrinthine path—through corridors, through workspaces where people were welding scrap or sorting materials, through mysterious labs—that I started to suspect Finder of choosing a deliberately confusing path.

At last, Finder ushered us through a large sliding door and into a room with high ceilings with a large, partially-assembled machine at its centre. Our materials had been delivered, some crates still on their cart, others open beside it. All around the room were small piles of circuit boards or strips of metal panelling, yet in spite of the clutter it was absolutely clinically clean.

'Onna,' said Finder. 'I have brought Luxorian and their crew.'

A woman popped her head out from behind the machine. 'Guests!' she said. She dropped the huge spanner in her hand and clapped her work-gloved hands together with a hefty *paff*, then rushed out to greet us with one hand outstretched toward me. Her hair was curly and storm-cloud dark. Her skin was dark umber, her eyes ocean-black.

'I'm Onna Lef,' she said, charging at me with such force that I skittered back a bit before I remembered that I'd fought a void horror only *hours* ago and this greasy-aproned human couldn't hurt me.

'Lux,' I said, extending a claw and letting her shake it.

'Oh, I know all about *you*,' she said, which was probably the most threatening thing ever said in such a friendly tone. 'Finder has been keeping me informed. We were looking for a long time for the right dragon for the job, you know.'

So smoothly I hardly knew how she'd done it, Vala was between me and Onna, who was forced to take a few steps back. 'What're you making?' she asked, hands on her hips.

Honestly, the idea of Vala protecting *me* was odd but sweet. She was so tiny...but then, my size had never protected me from the verbal barbs of humans. Vala had some kind of natural armour against those.

'You're not going to believe it,' said Onna. 'Actually...it's rather dangerous to know.' She glanced at Finder. 'I know you're all contractually obliged to silence, but you should know that we're not the first to work on this project. We were once part of a larger network of scientists and engineers, but two of our partners disappeared under mysterious circumstances, and the rest dropped the project either out of fear or outside pressure.'

I lashed my tail a few times to let out the nervous energy building inside me. I knew Finder had been keeping secrets but...disappearances?

'When you say disappeared,' Vala said calmly, 'I want you to be clear. Did they have reason to lose contact with you?'

'They did not,' said Onna. 'Nor did they have reason to lose contact with their loved ones. I check back in every few months, but they've been gone for over a year now. One of them left behind her husband and children.'

Rin wrung their hands. 'What are you involved with? If we've been collecting materials for...for a bomb, or, or a weapon...I don't want to know, okay? Tell me now, and I'll leave and I won't come back.'

Finder raised its hands in a calming gesture. 'Nothing like that! What we've made is for the betterment of dragonkind.'

Boro walked around the large device in the centre of the room. '*Dragon*kind?'

Finder walked over to me, gazing up at my face. 'I know you have wondered why I chose you specifically for the contract,' it said. '*This* is why. We have created a device to make dragons independent of humans, if they choose.'

I lashed my tail a few more times, my ears flattening as I tried to process this. Every few years, people came out with 'dragon-friendly' devices, not unlike my com. And not unlike my com, they were universally disappointing. Yes, I was glad I had my own com. When my grandparents had started work, they'd relied on their humans for all communications. But it was still a very limited help, still couldn't do everything a human com could do, still didn't address the fumbling dexterity of dragon paws versus human hands.

'How?' I asked.

Onna clapped her gloved hands together. 'You're going to love this. So—' She caught Finder's eye and the bot shook its head. '—ah, I'll let Finder explain.'

I looked at Finder. Though we'd travelled together for weeks, Finder had revealed none of its secrets until now. And, judging from the way Onna deferred to it, it seemed that more secrets remained.

Finder said, 'Are you familiar with the theory that dragons have mutable forms?'

I hesitated, parsing the words. I put one ear forward, one back. 'You mean...like how dragons all look different?'

'Adjacent to that, yes. Dragons do not conform to normal taxonomical classification. You consider yourselves one species, share culture, and interbreed, and yet some of you have scales, other feathers, others fur. Some have multiple pairs of wings, or multiple heads. There is even evidence of dragons with more insect-like qualities, like butterfly wings, though those are not well-documented.'

I perked my ears. I had never heard anyone discuss dragons from this sort of scholarly perspective. Or at least, not unless it was about our ability to soar the shining winds. 'Many creatures have variety,' I said.

Finder inclined its head. 'That is true. But none are recorded with as much variety as dragons—except perhaps bots. We are also mutable life-forms, but as inorganic constructs we are not easily comparable. But the mutable forms theory of dragons is that a dragon's form is not immutable, not simply that the species is varied. There are many human and dragon myths of dragons shapeshifting. That is closer to the mutable form theory.'

I snorted. 'You think dragons are shapeshifters?'

Finder shook its head. 'Biologists believe dragons may be *mutable*. Not necessarily shapeshifters, but not necessarily stable in form. Perhaps it has something to do with your ability to utilise faster-than-light speeds; the only other creatures which can even perceive your shining winds are the void horrors, which may or may not be the same species the way dragons are but certainly come in a great variety of forms.'

I frowned and couldn't stop my tail from thumping the ground heavily. Finder's point was valid, but I had never liked dragons being compared to void horrors. It was too close to the Cosmic Defenders' rhetoric that it was our duty to fight. It was also, frankly, uncomfortable to dwell on similarities with them.

'What does that have to do with dragon independence?' I said. I looked at the machine in the middle of the chamber, easily large enough for a dragon to stand in. 'Are you going to shape us hands like we're made of putty?'

'More or less!' said Onna cheerfully.

I fluffed my feathers up in alarm, barely able to take in what that meant.

Finder paused longer than usual and said, 'Onna's statement is misleading. Our device harnesses the mutability of dragons to give you a temporary humanoid form.'

Boro scoffed loudly. I looked around at the rest of my crew: Vala looked bored, and Rin stood utterly still.

'You must be joking,' I said, though I knew Finder wasn't.

It said, 'We had considered shrinking a dragon's size, and that's still an option, but found that in most models this was not sufficient to give a dragon full autonomy. Bots experience something similar when choosing our shells: we have greater access to society as humanoids than as any other shape.'

'We've built off the work of fabricators and clone technology,' said Onna. 'It's actually extremely similar and, we believe, quite safe.'

It made a kind of sense. Humans and dragons had been augmenting themselves for years, both with technology and biology. In that sense, *all* creatures were mutable.

But the difference between growing extra wings or cloning a hatchling and actually transforming one creature into another...I couldn't get my head around it.

What would it feel like to be human-shaped?

Did I want to be?

Rin asked something that got everyone talking, but their voices faded away as I sank into myself.

A dragon in human shape...

At some point, we made our farewells. I remember Vala's hand on my foreleg, guiding me out with a gentle touch. Someone must've arranged rooms for us because I fell asleep in a faded white chamber with a broad mattress and brown sheets.

I told myself I was angry.

I almost believed it.

Chapter Thirteen

My com beeped in the night. I snarled and dug it out of my nest of brown sheets. 'Tyroria' blinked on the screen.

Mum. She'd want to know how things were going.

My fire pouch stung and smoke curled from my nostrils. I rejected the call and burrowed deeper into the sheets.

The next morning, Boro knocked on my door. 'We're having breakfast at the street market,' he told me when I blearily let him in and collapsed back onto the mattress. 'Bas-Ros street market has some of the best food in the system, and it's cheap, too. Plus it'll be easy to find somewhere away from the crowds to eat.'

I knew that must be for my benefit. Boro loved crowds.

It also raised a new and frightening thought: our contract was over. We'd delivered the goods. Sar always had a big end-of-contract party where we'd say goodbye to our temporary crew or negotiate new contracts with them.

Was breakfast our crew's version of that? I was the boss; it was up to me to decide what we did and didn't do...but I couldn't keep anyone here who didn't want to stay. And Boro, like Sar, was a very traditional crewperson. He'd want the party, or some version of it.

Boro raised his eyebrows at me. 'Boss?' When I didn't respond, he hesitated. 'Lux? Can I help?'

I shook my head. 'I'll be out soon. Where are we meeting?'

'Lobby,' said Boro. 'Rin went to wake Vala; she was out drinking last night.'

'And you weren't?' I knew Boro liked a bar just as much as Vala. Probably more, since Vala only went for the drink whereas Boro went for the people, too.

Boro shook his head. 'I had too much to think about.'

My stomach sank. 'See you in the lobby.'

Boro frowned at me and opened his mouth as if to say something, then turned and left.

I puffed up, cold in spite of the lack of chill, and burrowed further into the brown sheets.

There was a dragon scrub-room and blessedly no other dragons present, so I quickly found a cramped shower and fluffed up my feathers, taking in all the soapy water I could before rinsing off and blasting on the heat. The water burned as it poured over my acid-scarred wings, shoulder, and face, still raw from my fight with the void horror.

As tight a fit as it was, I didn't come out looking my best. Normally, I'd have just carried on regardless—after all, it's not like I had Sar to complain anymore—but this time I took a moment to preen myself, smoothing my feathers and removing some of the soap that had built up on my wings where I hadn't had room to spread them properly.

Human scrub-rooms, I knew, had enough room for most humans. The thin ones, at least. Intellectually, I understood that dragons required much more space than humans. That our scrub-rooms were cramped, yes, but they were many times larger than the human ones.

I still wished the space wasn't so obviously begrudged. It wasn't enough. Somehow, it was never enough.

I shrugged on my pack over my head and made my way down to the lobby. It was familiar, in a dull way; much of last night was still a blur. My crew lounged in a circular booth: Vala with her head in her hands, Boro stretched out and comfortable, Rin with hands in their lap and shoulders tense.

'Finder?' I asked, then flattened my ears. Finder had the least reason to stay with the crew, and no reason at all to join us for breakfast.

'I messaged it,' said Boro. 'It is busy and sends its regrets.'

'Of course.' I couldn't still my lashing tail.

'Alright,' said Boro. He bumped his shoulder against Vala. 'Time to go.'

Vala lifted her head from her hands, revealing bruised, bloodshot eyes. She must have noticed my concern. 'Alcohol intolerance,' she said. 'It's getting worse but I'm not willing to give it up just yet.' She rubbed her face tiredly. 'Let's get this over with,' she said, and shuffled out the door.

I didn't feel much better as I followed her.

The street outside our stayhouse was quiet, with the noise and music of the street market pulsing in the distance. I steeled myself to the coming clamour; better than a party at a bar, surely.

To my surprise, Boro did not lead us into the heart of the market, where I could see a river of humans, dragons, and bots all bumping past each other, rubbing shoulders as they shopped, ate, laughed, or danced to the musicians playing lively drums and bell-organs in the streets. Instead we walked the outskirts until we came upon a large food-stall staffed by a wyrm with a thick fur ruff and a boxy bot with flaking red paint.

The dragon's ears immediately perked on seeing me. 'Hello, hello!' he crooned. 'Hot food for you and your crew? We also deliver to rigs!' He nudged the bot with his tail, who startled and said, 'ROTATING MENU TO KEEP THINGS FRESH. TODAY'S SPECIALS ARE ROAST MOOF AND QUALITY CHARGING PORT.'

'Quality charging port?' Rin stepped forward, examining the stall curiously. 'What makes it different from any other charging port?'

'AH,' said the stall bot. 'YOU HAVE SEEN RIGHT TO THE HEART OF THE MATTER. BOTS TYPICALLY USE WHATEVER CHARGING PORT IS AVAILABLE WITH NO

THOUGHT FOR THE SPEED OR QUALITY OF THE
CONNECTION, WHEN IN FACT DIFFERENT ENERGY
SOURCES AT DIFFERENT SPEEDS CAN PROVIDE AN
ENTIRELY DIFFERENT CULINARY EXPERIENCE.'

'Sounds like bullshit to me,' said Vala.

I hadn't noticed Finder expressing any preference...or any bot ever
expressing any preference, but perhaps they had just been being
practical, or polite.

The stall bot actually seemed to wilt a little, but the dragon touched
its shoulder with his muzzle in a show of support. 'It's not bullshit, it's
pioneering,' he said staunchly. 'It is only a matter of time until Buzzer's
Quality Charging Ports hit the mainstream. But in the meantime, as
there are no bots among you, perhaps I could interest you in the roast
moof? It comes with a drink and steamed vegetables.'

'Avva juice?' asked Vala, naming a common hangover 'cure'.

Rin wrung their hands together. 'Do you have a vegetarian option?'

Boro and I ordered the moof and I paid for our meals and
transferred enough credits to cover Rin and Vala as well.

There was a large courtyard here with a holo-fountain and various
human-sized seating scattered around it. I claimed a corner for us,
blocking it off with my body, and Boro settled across from me on a
sturdy bench, unwrapping his meal sack on his lap.

I placed my own meal on the ground, snipped the twine with my
claws, and spread out the thin cloth wrapping. The meal was in an easily
recyclable food case and as I popped the lid, steam and scent rose from
it, heady and pleasant. In fact, it was a pile of meat drizzled with gravy
and with a large cluster of purple veg on the side. It had been cooked
well, still just a little pink in the centre of each shred.

'This can't be actual moof, can it?' I said, though it certainly
smelled like it.

'Might have been imported from planetside,' said Boro. 'I doubt it
though. But synthetic is just as good.'

I lowered my head and seized a hunk of meat between my teeth. As the seasoned gravy and meat hit my tongue, I had to agree. 'I think this is dragon-flamed,' I said. 'Can you taste it?'

Boro frowned. 'Just tastes chargrilled to me.'

'Hmm.'

I looked at the food stall speculatively. There was a large spit and grill at the back of the stall, but I couldn't see how it had been lit or fuelled. Dragon-flamed meat tended to cook much faster and burn on the outside, but that was all the clue I had. It'd seem foolish of a dragon chef not to use their own flame, but I supposed there might be hygiene issues if it wasn't done right.

Vala and Rin arrived, each with their own meal sacks and Vala already swigging from a bottle. They took the seats either side of Boro and tucked into their own meals.

'So did they have Avva juice?' Boro queried.

Vala shook her head. 'That bot, Buzzer, ran and got me some from another stall.'

'Kind of it,' said Rin.

Vala shrugged. 'It got paid.'

'Did anyone catch the dragon's name?' I asked. I couldn't remember whether he'd introduced himself or it had been on a sign or something...I always forgot to ask until it was too awkward.

Vala shook her head and Boro frowned.

'Lyricos,' said Rin. 'His name's Lyricos.'

I nodded, thoughtful. Lyricos didn't have a human rider, nor did his job require one. A dragon cook...the closest I'd seen to it was Xax, and I doubted Xax ever dirtied her claws by cooking. Maybe Buzzer fulfilled a similar role to a rider...or perhaps they were just business partners.

After that, there was a few minutes of near-silence as we all tucked into our meals. Mine had come with a delightful spiced water, which made a good compliment to the gravy and meat. I drank it carefully from the large cup provided—we dragons rarely have lips as flexible as, say, a human, and it can make drinking from portable containers more than a little awkward.

As good as the food was, it couldn't completely distract me from the conversation looming over us. A conversation I knew that, as boss, it was my job to initiate. A conversation I desperately didn't want to have, because I knew I wouldn't like the answers.

Time stretched. I picked at my meal, not wanting to finish it and move on. I could feel Boro's gaze on me.

I sighed and shoved the remains of my meal away. 'Alright, crew,' I said. 'You did an amazing job. None of us had ever worked together before, but we worked together well. Rin, your technical and repair work was even better than I'd been led to believe, and your coms were always on-point. Boro, you held the ship together and kept everything ticking over. Vala, you kept us safe, never took security too far, and picked up rig work fast. And Finder—' I paused, and carried on, '—operated our tech with perfect efficiency. Now that our contract is up, none of you need to stay on.' I swallowed hard, my mouth suddenly dry. 'But I hope you will. All of you.' I rested my gaze on each of them in turn.

There was a long pause.

'Do we have another contract lined up?' Vala asked.

My ears drooped. 'No, not yet.' I'd thought the largesse of our first contract might buy me time to do so. 'And...I'll be honest with you, I doubt every contract I take is going to pay as well as this one. I still think Finder was short-circuiting to pay as much as it did.'

Rin tapped their lips. 'Finder always seemed very reasonable to me. If its device really works...' They trailed off and shrugged.

If its device really worked, then it and its partner would likely become incredibly wealthy. And might be the blueprint for even more technology. I'd never heard of anything like it.

I didn't know how to feel about any of that.

'Do you think you'll use it?' asked Rin.

My feathers fluffed in alarm. 'What?'

'Finder's device,' said Rin. 'Do you think you'll use it?'

I cast my gaze around the courtyard. A pair of bots chatted at the other side, one a wheeled bot with multiple arms, the other a humanoid bot. There was a trickle of people outside the courtyard—not through, since I took up a good amount of space—but it was far from crowded, and the pulse and noise from the nearby streetmarket was enough to drown out conversation.

There were no dragons here but Lyricos, his cheerful patter occasionally turning passersby into customers. Looking wholly incongruous for a dragon in his stained cook's apron as he curled around their food stall.

Or maybe not incongruous. Maybe that's what we'd all be doing if we weren't pushed to find riders and serve the Defenders or get a merchant rig.

What might I have become, if I had never had a rider? If I'd chosen my own path from the start?

What might I become now, if I never needed one again?

'I don't know,' I said at length. I looked down at my paws, curling my toes with each of their long claws. Each paw large enough to pick up a human. Too large for so much I wanted to do.

I definitely wouldn't want to be the first. Changing your body like that...it sounded painful. It also sounded like things could go badly, badly wrong.

What's more, with the threats they'd received, I wasn't sure how safe it would be *socially*. To be living proof of the technology, when their colleagues—including, I noticed, the dragons they'd been working with—had all been driven off.

There was just too much to think about. Too many variables, too many risks. It was tempting, but it was terrifying.

'We know independence is important to you,' said Rin. 'I hope you won't feel pressured into anything.'

'Yeah, you're already crushing it with independence,' said Vala. 'You're a real self-sufficient serpent.'

'Am I?' I said. 'I can't run this rig on my own. I still need a crew. And I needed help to scrub off the acid from the horror. I need help with so many things...'

'Everyone needs help,' said Rin. 'Why do you think we're here? None of us can do a rig contract alone. Not even Boro.'

Boro snorted.

I couldn't shake the feeling that they still didn't understand. That they couldn't. They could crew any rig, but me...

'I got lucky with this crew,' I said. 'I can't count on every crew to be this good.'

Vala yawned and leaned back on her seat. 'Well, I'm not going anywhere. This is the first gig that hasn't thrown me out for bad behaviour.'

Rin raised their eyebrows. 'Your behaviour isn't bad.'

'Mostly,' said Boro.

Vala bared her teeth at him. 'This is the first gig that hasn't driven me to bad behaviour. And I'm learning enough about running a rig that I might not have to do security forever, either.'

I looked to Rin and Boro. Both of them had originally considered me a potential dragon partner, not a boss. And while I wouldn't feel bad about that—I had never suggested otherwise, and they'd been very well compensated for the work—they would need to find another dragon to fulfil that.

Boro poked at the remains of his roast moof, but Rin tapped their chin thoughtfully. 'I can't promise I'll be here forever, but you're a good boss and this is a good crew. I feel like maybe we could be better than good, given time. I want to see what we'll become after more than a few weeks together.'

'I know you wanted to be a rider—' I started, but Rin shook their head. 'I want a lot of things.' For a blink, their face scrunched up in a way I couldn't name. Then they smiled. 'But the stars guide us to strange lands.'

I didn't doubt that they meant it.

Vala elbowed Boro. 'Well?'

Boro crumpled up his meal sack and set it aside. 'I came into this thinking it was a test to choose your rider.'

Vala rolled her eyes and Rin frowned.

I said, steadily, 'I know.'

'I know it wasn't, now. Much though I'd love to be your rider...you don't need one, if you don't want one. But me...' He rubbed the back of his head, ruffling his curly hair. 'I do still need a dragon partner.'

'Why, though?' asked Rin.

'I don't want to be alone,' he said, then waved away the protests of his crewmates. 'I know, I know—it's just different. It's different.'

It was different. Vala and Rin, who had never had a dragon partner, couldn't understand that. 'So you're leaving, then,' I said. I tried to keep my ears upright, tried to keep my voice level, but I couldn't quite stop myself from scraping my claws against the stone of the courtyard.

Boro nodded. 'Yeah. But...if you'll permit me to visit Tribute Fairs when they're about, I'd like to stay on until I'm chosen. This *is* a good crew and—' he grinned '—you'd all be lost without me.'

'It's true,' said Vala. 'Someone's gotta clean the rig.'

Boro elbowed her, which she accepted with a laugh.

I felt that laugh in my bones, an unexpected warmth. My crew were not going to leave me—not yet, at least. Not until we'd made a proper go of this dragon-led rig experiment.

This couldn't last forever. Nothing did. But just a little bit longer...that might be enough.

Chapter Fourteen

It was hard to find anywhere private in Bas-Ros Station, but I managed to climb up to a flat rooftop without bowling anyone over with my wings or tail, and I considered that good enough. It looked like this area was mostly used for storage, littered with crates and sacks. It was dusty as if from long disuse, and I hoped nobody was going to rush up to scold me.

I gazed down at the many passersby. A bot and a human strolled arm-in-arm. A furred wyrm walked sedately, three human children riding on their back while two human women laughed up at them. People pulled wagons, led pack animals, or even rode small vehicles carefully through the crowds. My gaze moved up to the street hanging above us which made an oddly distorted mirror: different buildings, different people, but somehow it all felt the same. I watched them for a while, enjoying the feeling of hanging upside-down, as if I'd rolled in the air. Wishing I could take off and stretch my wings.

At length, I pulled my com from my pack and commed my mother.

I waited several minutes before there was a crackle and her voice came through. 'Well?' she said. 'Is your contract over?'

I fluffed up my feathers and settled more comfortably on the roof. 'It is,' I said. 'It went well. I hadn't done materials collection before, but I quite liked it.'

'And your crew were all fine working with you without a rider?'

'They were.' My pouch warmed as I thought of my crew and their assumption that we'd continue working together.

What was it Rin had said? *I want to see what we'll become.*

I wanted to see that, too. But for all our conversation had been encouraging, I knew they must still have questions. Questions I...didn't know how to answer. Didn't want to think about.

'You don't sound entirely convinced,' said my mother. 'Are they stealing from you? Without a rider, I don't think a more intimidating approach would go amiss. Humans are useful but they are only small—'

'No, mum. They aren't stealing from me.' How they would even go about that, when we were gathering materials nobody wanted anyway, was a mystery to me. And I was hardly a fledgling. I was a dragon of thirty-five with fifteen years of rig experience. I'd notice if anything didn't add up.

'Then what's the issue? It sounds like it's all gone great. Wasn't it a big payout?'

'It did. It was.'

I asked my mother what she was up to—she was staying on one of her retirement villages on Sett, protecting their livestock from poachers—and let the conversation move on.

It was easier to think of other things.

《 》

'Are you certain?' asked Finder-X239. It stood within the curl of my tail as we considered the vast device it had built with its colleague. In spite of the many tables piled with tech and loose papers, in spite of the many crates laden with materials, the room seemed emptier than it had before. Maybe it was the lack of Onna's frantic energy.

'I am,' I said. 'For now, at least. I don't want to be a test case.'

'I don't wish that for you, either!' Finder said. 'I want you to be a partner in this.'

I shook my head. 'You need more dragons involved than just me. I know you said you had other contributors who were driven away, but that's...that's not good enough. Something this big, something this potentially galaxy-shaking, it needs as many perspectives as possible. As many *dragon* perspectives as possible.'

Finder was quiet for a moment. If I pricked my ears, I could just make out the faint hum of its motors. Finder was intelligent, but it was also thoughtful. And so time dragged a little before it said, 'You are right, of course. But discretion is still necessary. I am unsure of how to seek new contributors safely.'

I bit back my frustration, not quite able to stop my tail from thumping on the floor.

'Why are you doing this?' I asked it, unable to keep a growl from my voice. 'Why did you and Onna risk so much to make this device that apparently you can't tell anybody about?'

'I have dragon friends, much like you, who have sought independence from riders,' said Finder. 'With their input, Onna and I worked to make aids to make their lives easier and less reliant on riders, but it always came back to their size. Nearly everything in the galaxy is built to human proportions. They asked if we could make them smaller. It seemed impossible...until it didn't. When news of our project leaked, they were the first targeted, and the most viciously.' Finder paused. 'But we're still trying.'

'I don't want to be smaller,' I said, and my voice shook. 'I want being large to be accepted.'

Finder inclined its head. 'I'll think on what you've said.'

As I left, I found myself torn again. Tempted by what it offered, but hurt by it as well. When presented with the problem of dragons sharing the same spaces as humans, it had come to the conclusion that it was easier to transform dragons than it was to change human spaces.

That wasn't right. That *couldn't* be right.

And yet...if it really worked...?

Disgusted with myself, I returned to the stayhouse.

《 》

Later, I gathered my crew in the lobby to discuss possible leads for work. 'I know a handful of potential avenues,' said Boro. 'Zen and Lika on Ton. Fortiens here on Bas-Ros. The Lemian Trade Company on Vel-Tar usually take on independent merchant-rigs, too.'

I nodded, cringing inwardly. The Lemian Trade Company paid poorly for trade you could sell yourself with the right contacts. Everyone else Boro listed, I'd traded through with Sar.

Vala said, 'That all sounds good to me.'

'You must have contacts,' said Boro. 'We all know this isn't your first rig.'

Vala leaned back in her seat and frowned up at the ceiling. 'This *is* my first rig,' she said. 'And I don't have any contacts for this kind of work. No bridges I haven't already burned, anyway.'

'Maybe burn fewer bridges,' said Rin.

'Keep on like that and I'll burn this one,' said Vala.

'What about Rin?' asked Boro.

Rin shrugged. 'This is *actually* my second rig,' they said. 'I wasn't privy to trade secrets on my last one, so I wouldn't know where to start. Unless Finder has more work for us?'

Boro looked to me. 'You must have contacts.'

I shuffled my wings. 'I do.' Everyone was looking at me. Looking *to* me. I was the boss, afterall. Ultimately, it was my job to find us work.

But these were my crew. Friendlier to me than any crew I'd ever known. 'It was mostly Sar who dealt with them,' I said, my ears drooping. 'And I don't know what she's said to them about me.'

Rin sat up straighter in their seat. Vala's eyebrows perked. Boro frowned.

'Sar,' said Boro. 'Your former rider?'

Of course Boro remembered her name. He was too damned organised.

'Yeah,' I said, dreading what must come next. There was an odd tension running through my crew. I tapped my claws on the ground and flicked my tail repeatedly.

All this time, I had tried not to wonder what they must think of me, abandoned by my rider and choosing to go it alone. What defects they must see in me and think 'that's why she left'. To me, it felt *right* that a dragon ought to be able to forge a career on their own, but I couldn't deny that I had only come to this path because Sar had forced me to.

'You don't have to talk about it,' said Rin. 'If you're not comfortable contacting them, then we'll find another way.'

I perked one ear uncertainly.

'Rin and I could sound them out,' Boro said. 'Take the measure of them and make sure we undo any nonsense that rider did.'

Rin's mech landed on their lap. They stroked it. 'Only if you want us to, Lux.'

'You don't care that she left me?' I said. 'You don't care what I did?'

'What did you do?' asked Boro.

'It doesn't matter,' Rin said sharply.

Boro shrugged and leaned back in his seat. 'I know it doesn't. We all know Luxorian, and it's in the past, anyway.'

'I'd like to give that Sar person a piece of my mind.' Vala thumped her fist into her palm.

'Is your mind in your fist?' asked Rin.

Vala bared her teeth. 'Sometimes.'

They weren't mad at me.

They were mad at *her*.

It felt like an impossibility. I was so often furious with Sar, for so many things, and yet I couldn't with complete certainty say that if I met her again, I wouldn't beg for her forgiveness even though I didn't know what I'd done wrong.

But maybe I hadn't done anything wrong.

Maybe it didn't matter, even if I had.

This was my crew. And as they discussed finding work, it occurred to me that maybe total independence wasn't an option for me, but maybe it wasn't an option for anyone. I didn't need a human, or to *be* a human, but I needed friends and colleagues. I needed community.

And for the first time, I was taking steps to building one for myself, instead of being an accessory to Sar's.

'I'll send Rin and Boro the details of my contacts,' I said. 'I'd be grateful if you could sound them out, but I'd like to be clear that I'd like to meet with them.'

Boro nodded. 'Of course, boss.'

'We need to look into replacing Finder as well,' I said. 'It'll depend on the work we get. I'd like to do more extractions and survey work if we can.'

Rin nodded. 'A lot more scenic than merchant gigs.'

'Less people, too,' said Vala.

'Do you think Finder and Onna might have more work for us?' asked Rin.

I flicked my tail. 'I'm not sure,' I said. 'But I'd be interested in finding out.'

I could do this. I was starting again, but that didn't mean everything I'd done and learned was lost. And this time, I could shape my life into something *I* wanted.

And maybe it didn't have to be just me and a rig of humanoids, either. There were dragons I liked, and maybe could befriend. Maybe we could help each other, learn from each other. I thought of Xax and her pub in Lema-dar. Of Syranos, the kind merchant dragon I'd met after the dust storm. Of Lyricos the street food vendor, starting his own business with a friend.

I felt something unfold within my chest, electric and flowing. Not unlike the feeling of the shining winds.

Hope felt a lot like soaring.

Acknowledgements

I know I say this every time, but I wrote a very strange book. The concept I ran with was 'Dragons pull spaceships and are faster than light. And maybe shapeshifting will be an option for them. And the main character is a dragon!'

If you think that doesn't sound like a very professional starting point—well, that's me. However, it very quickly became a story about unresolved, broken relationships. About the hurt and paranoia of never knowing what you did wrong. About the frustration of being unable to be independent, but also the joy of how we do not exist alone and in a vacuum. And of course, about navigating a society that isn't built for you, and while I wrote that with fatness in mind, I'm sure it intersects very well with other experiences.

It was maybe a bit ridiculous of me to tackle such themes in a silly space dragons book, but I am a bit ridiculous myself.

As strange as this book is, I couldn't have published it without help. I'd like to thank my partner, Joh for believing in me and for providing so much helpful feedback. This book would look very different without their help. I'd like to thank Dona Vajgand, my incredible cover artist, for providing me with the most gorgeous possible cover with options on poses and ship design and all sorts of delightful things.

I'd also like to thank my Ko-fi supporters, both those who have opted to be thanked by name below and those who have chosen to go unnamed. I couldn't have afforded to publish this book without your help, and I wouldn't survive without your ongoing support. Your faith in me makes this all so much less scary.

Finally, I'd like to thank Merlin, my elderly cat, for purring beside my keyboard, screaming from the bed for me to take a cuddle break, and making sure I don't spend too long on my PC.

Special Thanks

It's odd to be officially 'self-published', because that's not the whole story. While I am not reliant on a mainstream publisher, I am reliant on my readers and supporters, folk who share and fund and review my books, both for the small things and the large.

And with that in mind, this book would not have been published without the help of the generous folk below.

I'd like to thank Aily Enne, Alex T. Dragonson, Alex Q, Anna, Anna, Azaliz, Bas van Haastregt, B. Kramer, chimerical girls, Cyberfossil, D. Moonfire, Flo Songweaver, FRAUD, gim, and Gwenfar.

I'd also like to thank HighlyCapyble, James 'Jubal' Baillie, Jon Kelly Hays, José Carlos Cuevas, josh g., katre, koalou, Lara Dufour, lilith, L. Rowyn, L.J., May Keable, Nex, Noé De Cuyper, Octobre, pawsies, pixin, Rachyl S., Rai Lionhart, RaiKa, Rebecca Södergren, Ri Guijt, Rob & Jenny Haines, Robin Swift, Samantha Rose, and Samantha Vente.

And I'd also like to thank Sara, Sarah Russell, Sasha Fox, sbbeasley, Scott Bryant, Sean M., Soblow Xaselgio, Socheata Chan, Sophie Jane, Steve M., StoryDragon, Tak!, Tapewolf, tea, Terri Oda, The Ninetailed System, Willard Goosey, and Zatty.

Your support truly means so much to me. I hope you enjoyed the book. There are more in the works!

Sign Up For Publishing Updates!

I have written a lot of books and I plan to continue! If you'd like to receive an email every time I announce or publish a new story and not at any other time, you can sign up for my publishing updates newsletter at the link below.

https://veocorva.xyz/publishing-updates/

Consider Reviewing This Book

Hello reader. If you enjoyed this book, please consider leaving a review. As an indie author with no backing by a publisher, word of mouth is the only way my books will find new readers. So please do consider leaving a review on your review site of choice, posting a few words about the book on social media, and telling a friend you think might enjoy it.

A review doesn't have to be a full and involved thing. It can be as simple as 'I really enjoyed this book!'

It can really make all the difference for me.

Also by Veo Corva

Space Dragons
Space Dragons: Luxorian's Crew

Tombtown
Books and Bone
The Beautiful Decay
Familiar and Flame
Tinker and Terror
Making Friends

Standalone
Non-Player Character
The Old Goat and the Alien

Watch for more at https://veocorva.xyz.

About the Author

Veo Corva writes things and reads things and reads things out loud, and sometimes they get paid for that, which is nice because it means they can feed their cat.

They live in Wiltshire with their partner and their furry familiar and as many books as they could fit in their small flat.

They are anxious and autistic and doing just fine.

Read more at https://veocorva.xyz.

Milton Keynes UK
Ingram Content Group UK Ltd.
UKHW031309091124
450874UK00014B/287

9 781739 474256